Y0-CZM-182

SPECIAL MESSAGE TO READERS

This book is published under the auspices of

THE ULVERSCROFT FOUNDATION

(registered charity No. 264873 UK)

Established in 1972 to provide funds for research, diagnosis and treatment of eye diseases. Examples of contributions made are: —

A Children's Assessment Unit at Moorfield's Hospital, London.

•

Twin operating theatres at the Western Ophthalmic Hospital, London.

•

A Chair of Ophthalmology at the Royal Australian College of Ophthalmologists.

•

The Ulverscroft Children's Eye Unit at the Great Ormond Street Hospital For Sick Children, London.

You can help further the work of the Foundation by making a donation or leaving a legacy. Every contribution, no matter how small, is received with gratitude. Please write for details to:

THE ULVERSCROFT FOUNDATION,
The Green, Bradgate Road, Anstey,
Leicester LE7 7FU, England.
Telephone: (0116) 236 4325

In Australia write to:

THE ULVERSCROFT FOUNDATION,
c/o The Royal Australian College of Ophthalmologists,
27, Commonwealth Street, Sydney,
N.S.W. 2010.

HER CAPTIVE CAVALIER

Whilst war rages between King and Parliament, Caroline Neville lives at her cousin's home, Waring Manor. When a troop of Cavaliers arrives at the manor-house one day, Caroline accidentally shoots their leader, Lord Robert Ashring. For the next few days, she tends the handsome Cavalier's wound and shelters him from his enemies. She knows she is putting herself in danger, but she soon realises she would follow him to the ends of the earth to keep him in her life . . .

LIVVY WEST

HER CAPTIVE CAVALIER

Complete and Unabridged

LINFORD
Leicester

First published in Great Britain in 1999

First Linford Edition
published 2001

British Library CIP Data

West, Livvy
Her captive cavalier.—Large print ed.—
Linford romance library
1. Love stories
2. Large type books
I. Title
823.9′14 [F]

ISBN 0–7089–9742–2

Published by
F. A. Thorpe (Publishing)
Anstey, Leicestershire

Set by Words & Graphics Ltd.
Anstey, Leicestershire
Printed and bound in Great Britain by
T. J. International Ltd., Padstow, Cornwall

This book is printed on acid-free paper

1

Caroline took a deep breath, leaned against the door jamb in an effort to support her trembling legs, and steadied her arm with her left hand. She pointed the wheel-lock pistol they always kept prepared, and prayed her voice would not betray her.

'If you venture nearer, I will shoot!'

To her relief her voice was firm. There were no tell-tale quavers to be mistaken for fear. If she was breathless it was the result of her minutes of frenzied activity. She had raced from the kitchen to get the pair of pistols immediately Joan brought the news. She was taut with effort, but also with fury that their peace should be disturbed.

The tall, dark man, his hand on the gate which gave entry to the privy garden in front of the long, low house, looked up in astonishment. His eyes crinkled in delighted amusement.

'I come on a peaceful errand, mistress,' he replied mildly. 'I do not wage war on children.'

She bristled with renewed fury. She was no child, and he should be made to learn that.

'Which is no doubt why your men rode through the village with no care for people they might run down!' Caroline retorted angrily. 'They are armed ruffians! You're no more than a troop of thieving vagabonds! We don't want your like in Winchworth. Be pleased to take them away.'

By now she felt able to move without support. She could even hold the pistol one-handed. She held it more firmly and took a step towards him, down on to the path outside the door. Jacob, with a muttered curse on all plundering soldiers, slipped out of the house to stand beside her, waving the other pistol which seemed, Caroline thought fleetingly, to threaten them more than the stranger.

'Will you not listen to me first?' the visitor said calmly. 'You, too, would look a trifle bedraggled had you ridden through the night, with little time to rest or eat, and no shelter against the storm.'

To her fury, Caroline found herself wavering. He sounded so reasonable, and it had been a fierce storm the previous night. They must be soaked. Then she thought of Peter and hardened her heart. They could let the sun, which was now high in the sky, dry out their miserable rags. She forced herself to recall what they were, and why they had to move in secret.

'I would have no cause to ride in such a clandestine manner!' she snapped.

'Clandestine? You have just accused us of lack of care,' he said, amused.

His smile was undeniably attractive, slightly lopsided and revealing perfect white teeth. He was the most handsome man she had ever seen. It merely aggravated Caroline's fury. She reminded herself that she had seen very few men with which to compare him.

'Now you mock me for an ill-chosen word! Soldiers, however they arrive, will find neither succour nor lodging here. We don't want you in Winchworth. Leave us in peace.'

Suddenly his amused tolerance faded. She was a beauty, with her big brown eyes, shapely form, and dark auburn hair that reminded him of beech leaves in winter. She was fiery and young, brave yet foolhardy, and in other circumstances he would have been tempted to dally, to try and turn that cool disdain into the fiery ardour her colouring promised. But his business would not wait. Much as he might have relished a few hours of dalliance, he had no time. He stepped forward.

'Stay there. Not a step closer or I shoot!' Caroline said swiftly, and trusted that the slight tremor in her voice would be put down to anger rather than fear.

And she was angry. It was fury which made her tremble slightly, not fear that he would call her bluff and force her to carry out her threat. Nor was it fear of the consequences if she did not succeed in preventing this invasion. She was only too painfully aware that two ancient pistols were a pitiful defence against a party of soldiers. Her only hope was that they would take her gesture seriously and look for a friendlier welcome elsewhere. But he ignored her and strode deliberately up the long, brick-paved path which divided the garden. He seemed oblivious of the threatening pistols aimed at him by the girl and a bent, old man who hovered behind her.

'Enough!'

His voice was one used to command, and for a fleeting second Caroline almost gave way. Then she thought of all they stood to lose, and gripped the pistol more tightly.

'Go away!' she repeated.

'I came peaceably to request aid for the King's men. And we pay for what we take. You have no fear of being cheated. I do not need your permission to quarter them in your barn for a few hours. It was but civility to ask. I expect to be treated with equal courtesy, not threatened as a miscreant!'

'They'm in the stable yard now, Mistress Caroline, dozens o' 'em. Horses all lathered an' eyes rollin'. Right fearsome lookin' brutes they do be!'

Joan's rich country burr, shrill with unaccustomed excitement, erupted suddenly from the dark hall behind her, and Caroline gritted her teeth. She didn't believe they paid for what they took. They had heard, even here in Winchworth, many miles from the battles which had raged over the rest of England, of the heedless depredations of both sides in this tragic conflict. She would never permit them to steal horses and fodder and take the grain stored from the recent harvest.

She and the other villagers had worked hard enough for what they had. Even if these men paid, and she had no real belief that they would, the farm and village could not afford the loss of horses and food. How would they survive the winter then?

She had no doubt they wanted the horses, whatever this fine stranger said. Horses had become more valuable then ever. There were too many stories of soldiers wandering the countryside, taking whatever they wished. All too often they paid nothing, or gave empty promises of future recompense.

'Shall I guard the kitchen door?' Jacob asked eagerly.

His cracked, old voice wavered uncertainly, though to Caroline's ear he sounded admirably determined and warlike. After all, he had been a seaman forty years before. He'd seen battles and killed men, if his tales were true.

'Stay here. We'll deal with this one first!' Caroline hissed at him.

She wasn't at all certain she could

maintain her defiance without some support, weak though Jacob's was. Aloud, she spoke to the steadily advancing man.

'I give you no further warning! Come just one step nearer and I shoot!'

There was a sudden guffaw from beyond the gate, and Caroline glanced towards it. She bit her lip. There were more of them than she had expected, four more here and heaven only knew how many at the back.

'No slip of a gal can shoot straight!' one of the men crowding round the gateway jeered.

'She'd miss the barn at that distance,' another agreed.

'She's a bonny enough piece. I'd give a week's pay to take her into a barn for an hour or so!' a third said, sniggering.

The man walking so steadily and relentlessly towards her, so tall and commanding, laughed.

'Enough, Saunders. You know full well such tasty wenches are mine first,' he tossed back over his shoulder.

Caroline's finger tightened on the trigger. How dare they! She had to confess inwardly to a moment of fear. He wouldn't dare! Yet they'd heard such tales. Perhaps he would. Her heart began a sudden uncontrollable thudding in her breast. Then she shook her head to clear it of stupid and fruitless speculations.

He couldn't possibly know she had never held the pistol before. Many women in these dangerous times had learned to shoot. He couldn't know it was Jacob who kept them primed and loaded, or that they were the only weapons in the house apart from an ancient, rusted sword belonging to Peter's grandfather. There were also, she recalled, a couple of muskets Peter had used for sport, but they needed skill and time to load, a skill and time they did not possess.

2

At that moment Joan screamed and Jacob's wife, Bessy, cowering in the hall, began to whimper and gabble frantic prayers.

'Mistress Caroline, they'm in the kitchen!' Joan cried, and screamed again.

Caroline heard the noise of heavy boots and the clink of metal on the stone-slabbed floor behind her. In desperation she pointed the pistol, shut her eyes, and pulled the trigger. The explosion made her jump, and she almost dropped the pistol.

An angry yell from the men at the gate made her open her eyes again. She was just in time to see the man on the path crumple slowly to the ground.

Pandemonium broke out. Joan and Bessy screamed in unison. Jacob, dancing about beside Caroline in a fever of indecision, loosed off his own pistol and the ball whistled past her ear to smack harmlessly into the stone wall surrounding the garden.

'She hit him!' a man shouted.

Sheer astonishment filled the man's voice, and for a few moments everyone stood still. Afterwards Caroline dreamed of that scene, every small detail imprinted on her memory. In the sudden silence she heard a bee in the roses which scrambled over the door. A bird trilled once, and in the far distance, somewhere in the village, a dog barked. In front of her, in her beloved garden which she tended so lovingly, her enemy lay alone and frighteningly still.

He sprawled across the path, his head cushioned on a bed of marjoram, one arm outflung to embrace a sturdy stem of angelica. Behind him, framed in the archway of the gate, his henchmen stared, mouths agape. A bright, red-skinned apple, the sweet, crisp ones she loved to eat, chose that moment to drop from its tree. It plopped with a small dull thud on to the path between his feet.

Caroline realised with a shudder of dismay that the same colour was seeping on to the dark green marjoram.

The almost still picture shattered then and at the same moment everyone moved. Joan began screaming hysterically, while Bessy berated her, and Jacob stammered petrified excuses and apologies. The men at the gate, overcoming their surprise, started forward but Caroline was nearer and faster. Long before they reached him she was kneeling beside the man she'd shot, feeling with anxious, trembling hands for the wound.

Her arms were seized unceremoniously and she was thrown aside. As she fell into the fragrant bed of mint, the men bent to examine their leader.

'You'll swing if you've killed his lordship, you hussy!'

One of the them spat viciously at Caroline, but she ignored his tone.

'Is he dead? Where did the bullet hit him? Where is he hurt?' she demanded urgently, struggling to her feet.

'Keep away, you little devil! You've done harm enough!' one snarled at her, as he bent over the fallen man.

Another, looking round helplessly, called angrily towards Bessy, wailing in the doorway.

'Cease your noise, woman! Prepare a bed for his lordship. Then rags and a bowl of hot water, and salves.'

Bessy responded at once to his note of command. She gulped back her tears and scurried away, shepherding Joan in front of her. Jacob hovered beside them as two of the soldiers lifted the wounded man.

'Show us a bed,' one ordered Jacob, and the old man, gabbling apologies and excuses, made haste to lead them inside.

Ignoring Caroline, they carried him carefully towards the house, and up the wide, wooden stairs to the main bedchamber, unused since Sir Peter left to go to the wars. Caroline followed the grisly procession. Had she killed him? She hadn't meant to, just to frighten them away.

She was vaguely aware of other men crowding into the hall from the kitchen, a dozen or more of them, staring and muttering, an ominous rumble. One of them took the pistol from Jacob's unresisting hand, and Caroline realised she had dropped hers somewhere.

Bessy had already spread a good linen sheet on the bed. The men laid their leader down gently, turning his head so that Caroline, pressing close behind them, could see the long wound which grazed his scalp. It was oozing sticky, bright red blood, his long dark hair already wet and tangled with it. She realised that he was still alive, and breathed a prayer of thankfulness that she hadn't killed him.

The men and Bessy, forgetting

enmity, worked briskly to staunch the blood and cleanse the wound. Bessy gave orders, her earlier panic forgotten in the need for action. One of the men tore up an old sheet he was handed, passing the strips to Bessy as she dabbed at the wound. Joan held the bowl of water, while Jacob busied himself fetching wood to build a fire in the grate, left cold and empty for so long, like Caroline's heart since Peter died.

Only Caroline had no task, and she sank down on to the wide windowseat, trembling as she watched. He wasn't dead. She couldn't have killed him. But that didn't mean that he would recover. She might still find herself guilty of murder. She started nervously when he moved, pushing Bessy's hand away from his head and struggling to raise himself.

'Confound you, Tyler!'

His voice was faint, but unwavering.

'Stop fussing over me like a mother hen!'

'Lie still, sir, do!' Bessy begged. 'That be a real nasty wound, and ye've been out of your senses, too.'

'A mere scratch,' he said, putting up a hand to feel the wound, and grimacing as he touched it. 'It will mend soon enough. Some pillows behind me, Tyler. I'll be damned if I lie here helpless. So, my pretty mistress,' he went on, turning to look at Caroline, 'you can shoot a pistol after all. It's fortunate you didn't aim for my heart, but were content with my head!'

Caroline stood up abruptly. Her fears for him changed at lightning speed into bitter anger.

'You don't think I meant to hit you, do you?' she demanded vehemently. 'I just wanted to frighten you! I wanted you to go away! I wasn't aiming at you, truly I wasn't!'

'Never trust a woman,' Tyler said with a grin. 'Especially with a gun!'

His master laughed.

'Not very flattering, to be told we're

not wanted in so decided a fashion. But, mistress, if this is the effect of your aiming elsewhere, methinks I'll take you back to the King's army. We could do with soldiers of your skill!'

3

Caroline's mood swung impetuously at the stranger's tone. Now it seemed she hadn't killed him, and from his remarks it looked as though there was no danger of his succumbing, her anger erupted. He was treating her as a child, not a woman of eighteen who had managed the house and farm for two years and more.

'You mock, sir!'

She glared at him as he lay propped against the pillows, his head bandaged, but his eyes, unusual eyes, she noticed, brown with flecks of gold, were gleaming with amusement at her discomfiture. Before she could continue he waved Bessy and his men away.

'Go, please. Leave me alone, all of you. The noise you make disturbs me. The lady shall remain and entertain me awhile.'

He turned to smile at Bessy.

'Thank you for your care, mistress. I wonder if you could do me yet more honour? My stomach tells me it is long past time for breakfast.'

'Dearie me, have ye not eaten this morning?' Bessy demanded, her housewifely instincts roused.

'We were to eat when we'd found somewhere to sleep for an hour or two,' one of his men replied. 'We have bread and meat. We won't be thieving from your larder,' he added, glancing at Caroline. 'We have sufficient for our needs. But his lordship might appreciate something.'

'Of course he would, the poor man! He needs broth and a few morsels of chicken. I'll see to it at once, while Jacob shows you the barn and where to water your horses.'

'My thanks,' their leader intervened. 'Go with him, Tyler, and the others. We can only afford a couple of hours. Don't forget to set a guard.'

Tyler hesitated, gesturing doubtfully

at Caroline. The man in the bed laughed.

'I don't think you need worry any more about my safety. She has no more weapons with which to slay me, unless she chooses to use her lovely eyes! Our gallant former adversary shall keep me company to ensure no further harm comes to me. Go and see that the men are all settled.'

Caroline watched, bemused, as Bessy and Jacob bustled out of the room, eager to give this audacious man their best attention. And their best food, no doubt, as he'd been given the best bed in the house, that no-one else used. Their enemy! One who would still no doubt rob them of whatever he chose.

'I begin to wish I'd hit you a little farther towards the centre of your arrogant head! Then it would have been one plaguey soldier the less to house and feed!' she said resentfully the moment the others departed.

'Are you too ignorant to understand what would then have become of you and your household?' he demanded with sudden brusqueness. 'Aye, and to the entire village like as not, if my men had chosen to take revenge! To say you didn't mean to aim at me would have availed you little then!'

Caroline shivered. She hadn't had time as yet to think of this, but she had a sudden, horrifying vision of the way his men would have treated her and the servants she was responsible for, all because she had tried to protect them. These rough soldiers would have spared no-one, not even poor old Bessy. Whatever they did to her she'd asked for, but they would in all likelihood have burned the village, raped the women and killed the men.

She'd heard tales of babies being roasted over a spit, and felt a moment's thankfulness that James was safely away with his uncle in Falmouth. Not that he was a baby any more, but he was too young to suffer for her instinctive, thoughtless actions.

She realised with a bitter wave of

helplessness sweeping over her that her puny resistance had been pointless. She could not have defeated professional soldiers, even if there had been no more than three or four of them. She might have led faithful Jacob to his death, and then what would have become of Bessy and Joan?

'I'm sorry,' she whispered at last. 'I just wanted to stop you taking our horses. Without them we can't work the farm, and if you take our food how will the villagers live this winter?'

'I need no horses, nor food,' he said, wearily resting his head against the pillows. 'As it happens we have enough. We're heading as fast as we can for Bristol, where Prince Rupert is besieged by Fairfax and has too few men to hold the defences. Horses are of no use except to get us there.'

'You are the King's man?'

'I am. I'll have no truck with rebels.'

'We hear the King is losing many towns,' Caroline said quietly, then wished she had not.

She had a sudden, inexplicable desire to see him smile, to soothe that worn frown from his brow. He looked tired and defeated, and she didn't know why she should care. She supported neither side, blaming them all for bringing war and death and misery to the country, involving innocent people who cared not a jot who ruled them up in London so long as they were left in peace to till their own land.

'Bridgwater and Bath have fallen, and Sherborne Castle,' he said, breaking into her puzzled thoughts. 'We hold Cornwall still, but that's no thanks to the leaders. Goring is drunk half the time and the rest always quarrelling.'

Before she could reply, Jacob came into the room bearing a flagon of ale and a pewter tankard.

'No doubt you'm thirsty, my lord,' he said, and handed the tankard, brimming, to the man in the bed. 'This be our best ale. My Bessy brews it herself.'

'Be careful, Jacob! It's too full!'

Caroline hurried to hold it, fearing

the patient was too weak to manage. He sank back, an odd expression in his eyes, and permitted her to hold the tankard to his lips.

'I thank you.'

He took a sip, then a longer swallow.

'Jacob, isn't it? Tell Bessy this is the best ale I've tasted for many a long day.'

Jacob, bending low, backed out of the room, a foolish grin on his face, and Caroline wanted to shake him. They were still enemies, these men who had pushed in uninvited.

'And you are Mistress Caroline, I believe? I am Lord Ashring, Robert Ashring, at your service.'

She knew she should have curtseyed, but she was leaning over the bed towards him, half sitting on it. And, she reminded herself hurriedly, he was neither a friend nor an invited guest. She was trapped by the tankard she held steady as he put his strong, lean brown hand over hers and kept her imprisoned. A slow blush stained her cheeks, and spread down her neck. It grew deeper as she saw his gaze slowly follow its progress, his lips curving into a slow smile.

'Mistress Caroline Waring?' he asked. 'This is Waring Manor, I was told.'

'It is,' she replied hurriedly, furious with her body for betraying her confusion so clearly. 'But I am not a Waring. The manor belongs to my cousin, James. His mother was my father's sister. My name is Caroline Neville,' she managed, her words disjointed, and her voice hoarse with embarrassment. 'Have you finished with the ale or would you like more?'

He gently pushed away the tankard.

'I have enough for now, thank you. Perhaps later. Will you stay with me and help me to eat?'

He smiled, an undeniably attractive smile. His mouth was firm and his lips full but not fleshy. And the gold flecks in his eyes seemed to sparkle more brilliantly when he smiled.

Caroline was shaken out of her

speculations as Joan appeared with a tray, and Caroline jerked her hand away and went to set the tankard down on the chest.

Bessy had produced a feast fit for a king at five minutes' notice, Caroline thought sourly. As well as the broth she'd promised there was a plate of cold meat cut finely, a wedge of rabbit pie, and a bowl of fresh gooseberries topped with thick, delicious yellow cream straight from the dairy.

'Shall I help to feed your lordship?' Joan asked hopefully, simpering and bending over unnecessarily far as she placed the tray on his knees.

Caroline felt an unreasonable spurt of anger as she noticed the girl was, as so often, untidy. The strings of her bodice had somehow come untied, and it gaped indecorously.

'I will attend to his lordship,' Caroline said curtly.

If she left him alone with Joan she'd probably find the wench in bed with him in no time, she thought, and that was no way to comfort a man who'd just been shot in the head! Joan gave her a sly look, then shrugged her shoulders, almost dislodging one insecurely anchored sleeve.

She turned with an unnecessary vehemence and walked slowly from the room, her rump swaying provocatively.

Caroline turned back to Lord Ashring. He lay with his eyes closed, the food disregarded.

'My lord? Will you not eat?'

He opened his eyes and sighed.

'I suppose I must, but I find I am no longer hungry. Odd, I was ravenous a short while since.'

Patiently, as though she were coaxing a child, Caroline fed him a few spoonfuls of broth. After a minute or so he shook his head and pushed away the bowl.

'I'm sorry, I cannot. I must sleep. It was a long and wet ride last night. In a couple of hours I shall be fit to ride on with the men.'

But he was not. Caroline sat and

watched as the first peaceful sleep turned into restless tossing, and then feverish ramblings. The wound must be more severe than any of them realised, for within two hours he was feverish, incoherent and quite unaware of where he was. He did not recognise Caroline or Bessy, and did not even seem to know his lieutenant, Tyler, who had been summoned hastily by Jacob from his rest in the barn.

'Best bleed him,' Bessy said calmly. 'I'll send Joan for the apothecary.'

'No point,' Jacob reminded her. 'He'll be away at his brother's in Barnstaple. It's his niece's wedding day.'

'Then there's no help for it. I'll have to do it myself,' Bessy declared assuredly.

The cupping, which Caroline could not bear to watch, so guilty did she feel, brought Lord Ashring to his senses for a short while. He tried to rise, but was too weak to stand.

'Tyler?' he asked, his voice scarcely

audible, looking vaguely round the room.

'I'm here, my lord.'

'Take the men to Bristol. His Highness needs them. And the letters. Tell Prince Rupert I'll be with you as soon as I am better. In a day or so.'

'Don't you worry, my lord,' Tyler replied efficiently.

'No, you're to stay in bed until you're well,' Bessy added.

Tyler went on, 'Bessy here'll take good care of you, and you get yourself fit before you try to ride all that way. I'll leave your horse. Jacob will care for him. Would you like one of the men to stay, act as messenger, belike?'

Lord Ashring shook his head, and winced.

'A plague on this stupid wound! No, take everyone. They're needed in Bristol more than here. Go as fast as you can, and let's hope you get there in time.'

Within hours, he relapsed into fever

and delirium, but Tyler and the men had gone.

Caroline, Joan and Bessy took turns to sit with him during the days that followed, bathing his brow with cool lavender water, and persuading him to sup milk or broth when he had a few moments of lucidity.

One of the old women from the village came to sit by his side at night, for, as Bessy said, the old crone could sleep during the day but she and Mistress Caroline had too much to do in the time that was left from nursing. They needed their sleep.

Caroline, blaming herself bitterly for his illness, slept fitfully and developed dark rings beneath her eyes. In the dark hours she tossed and turned in her bed, desperately afraid that she might, through her impetuous behaviour, be the cause of a man's death.

'Cheer up, Mistress Caroline. You didn't mean to hit the fellow,' Jacob said one day.

Joan was sitting with Lord Ashring

while Bessy baked bread, a task she would permit no-one else to undertake. Caroline had wandered out to the stables, too restless to remain in the house. She fondled the head of his lordship's horse, a powerful but gentle beast, and rested her forehead against his velvety nose as Jacob rubbed down his flanks with a wisp of hay.

'What difference would that make if he dies?' Caroline demanded petulantly.

'I thought you'd no time for either side, Mistress Caroline,' the old man said, squinting up at her.

'I thought so, too, but it's different when you know someone, especially when you've nearly killed them!'

* * *

In the middle of September, news came that Prince Rupert, under fierce attack from the Parliamentary troops at Bristol, had negotiated terms for the surrender of the city to Fairfax, and marched out to rejoin the King at

Oxford. Caroline was sitting beside the fire in Lord Ashring's room, staring at the flames and wondering dully what effect this might have on the progress of the war, whether it would soon be over, when she heard a muffled curse from the bed.

She leaped from the stool, knocking it over in her haste, and ran across to find Lord Ashring conscious. His eyes were wide open, and he had a puzzled look on his face.

'Where the devil? Caroline? Isn't that your name? I seem to recall that's what they called you. Why can't I move? I feel weak as a newborn babe.'

'You're better! Oh, thank God!'

It was with the greatest effort that Caroline fought back the tears of relief threatening to overwhelm her. Her hand trembling, she laid it on his brow and found his skin cool to the touch.

'Better? Have I been ill?'

Suddenly he chuckled.

'Oh, now I recall. You shot me! But it was just a scratch, not sufficient to make me feel so feeble and helpless!'

'You were very ill, with a fever, and I thought you'd never get better!' Caroline told him, her voice uncertain as she struggled with the relief she felt.

He laughed again, his voice faint, but there was genuine amusement in it.

'Did you fear you'd be branded a murderer?' he asked slowly. 'Is that why you were afraid?'

'No! Yes. I mean, well, of course I didn't want to be a murderer,' Caroline stammered. 'It wasn't just that. I didn't want you to die,' she whispered.

Somehow he'd caught her hand in his, and despite his weakness it was a firm grasp. She couldn't get away, she daren't pull too hard and hurt him.

'Why not, Caroline? Why do you care whether I die or not?'

4

Caroline shook her head as she replied, 'I have no desire to kill men,' then a note of anger crept in. 'Not like men who can do no better than make war!'

'You seemed very prepared to kill me when we first met,' he said softly. 'How long ago was that? Two days? The men went on without me, I suppose.'

'Yes, you ordered them to go to Bristol,' Caroline said, trying to release her hand, but his grip on it tightened.

'How long have I lain here helpless?'

'I never really wanted to kill you!' Caroline protested. 'It's just I detest all soldiers, everything to do with war! It has cost me, and everyone, so much,' she amended swiftly. 'Could you eat something?' she added on a softer tone.

She had no wish to answer his questions. He would fret himself back into illness if he learned too soon that

Bristol had fallen, and she could not bear to examine her own feelings closely.

Why did it matter, apart from her natural desire not to have killed anyone?

This quarrel of King and Parliament had ruined many lives. It had ruined hers by taking Peter's. It had almost made her a murderer. Yet this loss and the guilt she felt were pale emotions compared with the surge of relief and joy she'd experienced when Lord Ashring had come to his senses.

'I'll see what Bessy can find,' she said when he did not reply, and he released his grip on her hand so that she was able to escape.

Every day, Bessy prepared delicacies to tempt his lordship's appetite, and today she had a herb-flavoured chicken broth simmering on the kitchen fire. When Caroline told her the patient was awake, the fever subsided, she insisted on taking up a bowl of the broth and seeing for herself.

Caroline was happy to let her go. But it was a brief respite and she had not composed her thoughts before Bessy was back, declaring gruffly that invalids were always crotchety.

'Nothing will do for his lordship but that you act nurse and feed him,' she said crossly, but a smile trembled on her lips.

Caroline frowned.

'Why can't the stupid man feed himself? He seems strong enough,' she added, recalling his grip on her hand, and then blushed as she realised what she had said.

Bessy didn't appear to notice anything amiss.

'It's a good sign, shows he's on the mend, if he feels fit enough to go making demands,' she said.

So Caroline had to attend him, but to her relief the slight effort of consuming the broth exhausted him, and he fell into a deep but peaceful sleep as soon as he had finished.

* * *

For several days he was very weak, unable to talk much, but in the end Caroline had to face his questions. It was the first time he sat out of bed. Jacob brought a large chair up to the bedroom, and Bessy fussed busily, arranging cushions, and making sure he was not sitting in a draught.

'You can sit here by the fire,' she told his lordship, bustling round happily.

He had other ideas.

'Please move the chair to the window. I haven't been able to see outside while I've been a-bed, and prefer to have a different outlook for an hour or so.'

'But it's bitter cold outside, a nip in the air to show winter's coming,' she protested.

'I shall be swathed in dozens of shawls like a sickly baby if you have your way,' he said with a rueful laugh, indicating the pile of clothes she had ready.

'The draught! You might catch a chill!'

'I shall benefit from a breath of fresh air, and I can move back to the fire if it is too cold,' he said firmly.

It was the first time he had used that decisive voice, and Bessy responded to the note of unconscious authority.

'You have a beautiful valley,' Lord Ashring said sincerely a few minutes later.

Jacob and Bessy had been persuaded to leave, reassured he would come to no harm, and Caroline was alone with him. She had seated herself beside the fire, but he twisted round to look straight at her and gestured to her to come closer. She tried as hard as she could to avoid his eyes.

'Bring your stool here and sit beside me, where we can both look out of the window.'

Caroline was reluctant, but his tone commanded her. She moved the stool, setting it down as far away from his chair as it would go, almost against the wall. She turned back to the table beside the fire to pick up the embroidery she'd occupied herself with during the many hours she spent with him.

To her dismay, as she returned, she saw that he'd reached over and pulled the stool closer to his chair, so close that her skirts would be touching his legs as he sprawled beside her. Gritting her teeth to still the trembling, she sat down and tried, unobtrusively, to edge farther away. It was impossible so she attempted to concentrate on the chair cover in her hands.

'I love the valley. This house has been my home since my parents died ten years ago.'

'You must have had an aunt or guardian. You did not live here alone, surely.'

'Lady Waring was my aunt, my father's sister.'

'Yes, I recall you said something about that, before I grew feverish. She died?'

'Two and a half years ago, a few

weeks after Peter.'

'Peter?'

'My cousin. He was killed, at Braddock Down. She had been ill for a year or more, and it almost broke her heart when he insisted on leaving home. Afterwards she just didn't want to go on living, not even for little James's sake.'

'James? I don't recall hearing the name. But I am so hazy about events while I have been ill, I could have missed it.'

'He isn't here. He is Peter's brother. He's only eight, and when my aunt died he went to live with his uncle, his father's brother, in Falmouth. He shares a tutor with his cousins.'

'Why did you not go, too? I would have thought it preferable for a young girl to live in a town, with lively company, than alone here in an isolated village.'

'I preferred to look after the farm. Someone had to, and I felt it was my duty to Peter's memory. Besides, I do not especially like Mr Henry Waring, and he resented me. He was happy enough to agree,' she added drily.

'So your cousin died in the war, and your aunt. I can understand your dislike of all to do with it. But I've had no news, and Jacob tells me it's a month since I came here. What is happening in Bristol? Have you heard?'

'I'm sorry. It's bad news,' Caroline said gently, and at the bleak look in his dark eyes she would have given her very soul to be able to change the facts.

She reached out and laid her hand on his arm.

'Well?' he asked sharply. 'Come, it won't improve with keeping!' he added when she did not reply.

'Prince Rupert surrendered Bristol,' she said baldly, with no way of softening the blow.

For a moment she thought he had not heard, he was so still. Then he abandoned his relaxed posture, and started to push himself out of the chair.

'My lord! Don't! You're not strong

enough!' Caroline cried, dropping her embroidery and catching his arm.

His body was stiff with what Caroline guessed was anger and frustration.

'I don't believe it! Rupert vowed to hold Bristol! It's our only good port! The news is wrong. It must be.'

He sank back into the chair and clasped her hand, crushing it between his own.

'It's true,' she said quietly, wishing she could wipe the bleak, stricken look from his sad eyes. 'No-one knows why, but there are many rumours.'

'Rumours?' he demanded. 'Rumours about the surrender? Then it may not be true!'

'I didn't mean that. It is true. No, there were rumours about why he did it. Some say he hadn't enough men, and surrendered in order to prevent more deaths. Fairfax permitted him to march out and go to Oxford. But others — '

She stopped, biting her lip. She hadn't meant to say anything more, but their closeness, the tingling that gripped her as he held her hand, seemed to have driven out her commonsense.

'Well? Tell me the worst. I am used to his enemies spreading evil about him. What are they saying?' he demanded as he sat there staring straight at her, waiting for her answer.

'They are saying that he was bribed!' she whispered, and waited anxiously for his reaction.

To her relief he laughed. It was a bitter sound, but better than the blank, withdrawn expression.

'What rubbish! Rupert cannot be bribed! I've known him as a good friend for years, fought beside him, and know that all he cares for is to save the King. How can they accuse him of such nonsense? It's another trick of the Parliament.'

'It's not just his enemies, from what we've heard. The King's men are saying it, too. You see, while he and Fairfax were at Bristol, Parliament granted some money. I don't know the details, but it was a great deal, I believe, granted to his brother.'

'But the Elector Palatinate has been a pensioner of Parliament for years! That could not influence Rupert.'

'It's what they say,' Caroline said helplessly.

She was afraid for some reason. If he did not believe her, he might ride into danger. His next words seemed to confirm that fear, and her heart chilled.

'You say he's gone to Oxford? I must get well and join him there as soon as possible.'

'You can't,' Caroline protested. 'You're not strong enough,' she added quickly.

'Not now, but I will be soon.'

Caroline bit back her reply, and tried to turn the conversation. He made an effort to be polite, and listened to her description of how she had learned to manage the farm. To her relief, he soon tired and went willingly back to bed, but she knew he was thinking about it, making plans, by the abstracted expression which became so familiar during the next few days.

It was, however, several days before he spoke of it again. He was by then strong enough to come downstairs, and they were taking advantage of an unexpectedly warm day to sit in a sheltered spot in the privy garden.

'I see you had a visitor yesterday,' he said suddenly. 'A Parliamentary soldier, if I'm any judge.'

Caroline glanced at him uneasily.

'John Culham. He was one of Peter's friends. He was wounded slightly, and has been sent home to Barnstaple. He called in to see how we fared.'

'I hadn't realised your Peter was with the rebels. But he brought news?'

She nodded unhappily and hesitated before going on, still trying to sidestep giving him the news he waited for.

'Peter was disturbed about the way the King treated Parliament. He thought the squires, the landowners, should have more say in how they were taxed. He'd been planning to enter the

Commons, one day, you see.'

'I see, my dear Caroline, that you are trying to avoid giving me news. I'm not concerned with your cousin's beliefs, but with the situation today.'

Caroline sighed.

'Very well,' she answered after a few moments' hesitation. 'But I don't know if it's true. We hear so many conflicting things. Apparently the King dismissed Prince Rupert and ordered him to leave the country. He also arrested Colonel Legge, who was the Prince's friend, and replaced him as Governor of Oxford.'

There was a moment of stunned silence, then Lord Ashring spoke harshly.

'Is this true, or is it a rumour spread by those damned Roundheads?' he demanded.

Caroline sprang to her feet, distressed at the bleak look on his face, and tried to cover it with anger.

'I don't know! I can only repeat what I've been told! Why do you always question it? Why do you think I'd be telling you falsehoods? How can I know what is happening in Oxford, or anywhere else for that matter? I haven't been there! And I don't want to go there, or anywhere but here. I want to live in peace! I despise every one of you! You've taken Peter away from me with all this stupid fighting, and it's nothing to do with us.'

Blinded with tears, shaking her head to dispel them, she turned and took a hasty step away from him. But her progress was halted as he grasped her arm in a relentless grip.

'Caroline, my dear, I didn't mean to hurt you,' he said softly, and forced her to turn and face him. 'Of course I believe you're telling the truth about what you've heard.'

She blinked hard.

'Why should I try to invent untruths? What good would that do me?' she said in a soft, concerned voice.

He took her chin gently in one hand and forced her to turn and look up at him.

'None at all. But if it comes from this Culham fellow, a Parliament man, can you believe him? Don't you see, it's just the sort of rumour they would spread?'

Caroline tried to twist her head away. Standing so close to him, her arm still gripped with one hand, and his face so close to hers, made her feel weak and slightly uncomfortable.

'What good do they think it would do, to spread untruths?' she asked.

'I've known Prince Rupert for years, my dear, and it just isn't possible he'd become a traitor. Although he has enemies at Court, men who in the main are jealous of him, he is the ablest commander the King has. Without him the cause would be utterly lost. That's why I find it incredible the King would desert him.'

'John said Rupert was trying to reach the King, who was in Wales when it all happened, and by now might be anywhere,' Caroline muttered. 'Now, please, let me go as you are hurting my arm.'

He released her immediately, but she did not move. Slowly he took her face in his hands again and inexorably forced her to look up at him. There was hurt in her eyes, as well as anger.

With a gentle finger he brushed away a tear which trembled on her long lashes, and then pulled her to him, his arms urgent as they encircled her.

'I'm a brute. I shouldn't have let my surprise affect you, my dearest Caroline. My little love, I can't bear to see you so unhappy. Say I'm forgiven.'

She was trembling, for she had never before been so close to a man. Not even Peter had done more than give her a brotherly hug. She was afraid, but at the same time realised this was something she had been waiting for, since the moment she'd seen him lying unconscious on the bed, blood streaming from the cut on his scalp. Maybe, her thoughts whirled uncontrollably, since she'd seen him entering the garden where they now stood.

As he bent to kiss her she sighed, trustingly offered up her lips, and without thought raised her arms to clasp him tighter.

5

For several days Caroline lived in a haze of delight. She and Robert, as he insisted she called him, spent most of their time together. On mild days they walked in the garden, and as he grew stronger she showed him her beloved valley.

Hand in hand they explored the tracks which led northwards, away from the village and the fertile fields, leading eventually to the bleak uplands of the moor. For her, the present enchantment was enough. She gave no thought to the future.

She spoke of parents she could barely remember, and her home in Cornwall, left ten years ago. She told him, hesitantly, about the childhood betrothal with Peter and the sorrow of his early death. At first they did not talk of politics.

Caroline was reluctant to introduce it after her outburst, and Robert, she thought, refrained because he did not wish to distress her by arguing. However, she knew he gleaned news from Jacob, who got it from the villagers.

But one day he was so preoccupied she had to ask what he'd heard. They were sitting in the oak-panelled parlour Lady Waring had used when the family had no guests. It was a small, cosy room, and outside it was a cold, blustery October day.

'Bad news, I fear. Cromwell sweeps all before him in Hampshire and Wiltshire. The King is losing his last strongholds. And no-one seems to have the slightest notion of what Montrose is doing in Scotland,' he said heavily.

'Have you heard where Prince Rupert is?' Caroline asked.

She rose restlessly, and went to look out of the window at the rain beating down.

'Has he left England?' she insisted on

asking when Robert did not reply to her query.

'No,' he replied eventually, but in a voice heavy with emotion. 'He hopes to persuade the King to hear his side of events at Bristol. The King is at Newark, I believe, and Rupert will try to reach him there. Caroline, I'm well enough now to rejoin the army, what's left of it! I must go within a few days.'

Caroline stared at him, at first too surprised to speak. This had been a fear she had suppressed, something she could not, would not think about. Then dismay engulfed her and she held out her hand in mute supplication.

'My dearest Caroline!'

He pulled her gently into his arms, cradled her on his knees, and found she was shivering uncontrollably. He kissed away her tears, explaining he had a duty as a soldier.

'I long to stay here with you. You have cared for me so lovingly. It's been a few stolen weeks, a joyous memory I shall always treasure, but I must rejoin the King. He needs every man possible, and Rupert needs friends at Court, too, to counter the jealousies of men like Digby. You must try to understand how I feel.'

'And afterwards?' Caroline asked tonelessly. 'What will you do then?'

'It depends on what happens in the next few weeks, but it's not hopeful. It looks highly probable I'll be seeking my fortune in France or the Netherlands!'

And what of me, Caroline longed to ask, but dared not. It was abundantly clear to her that these few weeks which had been so momentous for her were incidental to his purpose in life. All he cared about was the King and his cause.

'I wish you well,' she said as lightly as she could. 'Now it's almost dinner time and I must help Bessy.'

She kept busy and out of his way for the rest of the day, and escaped early to her bed. She needed to be on her own, to have time to think.

It was inevitable, she told herself

bitterly, that she would fall in love with such a handsome young man when she'd been thrown into his company for so long, nursing him, especially when his illness was the result of her impetuosity. And yet, what was love?

She had no-one to ask. Could she possibly know herself?

It was equally inevitable, she told herself angrily, that he, for amusement during the time he had to be in Waring Manor, should seek diversion with her. Were not all men the same? And like a fool she hadn't seen it was simply a game for him.

She struggled to be fair. He had never mentioned a future. His tender endearments, his warm and exciting kisses which produced such strange and delightful sensations deep within her, might be nothing more to him than the casual greeting kiss everyone used. How was she to know what was normal behaviour amongst grown men and women of his type?

She had been just sixteen when her

aunt had died, and since then had never been in company except for one brief visit to Falmouth. Apart from the villagers, she knew very few people, just the occasional old friend from Peter's schooldays, men like John Culham.

She'd read far more into Robert's behaviour than was meant, and no doubt he would be horrified if he discovered the dreams she had been harbouring — dreams of always being with him, ridiculous fantasies which ignored all practical details, and went no further than the desire never to be separated from him.

* * *

It cost Caroline dearly to present a bright and cheerful face to the household the following day. Fortunately they were all busy picking apples and she had the perfect excuse to avoid Robert's suggestion of walking up on to the moor. But she could scarcely refuse the offer of his help in the orchard.

'When do you plan to leave us, my lord?' she asked briskly as she handed him a full basket to carry back to the apple store. 'Will it be before we have gathered the fruit?'

'You'm leaving?' Jacob asked, overhearing. 'It's too soon. You'm not properly well yet.'

'Well enough to sit in the saddle, and by the time I get to Newark I shall be quite my normal self. I ought to go tomorrow. Is my horse in good fettle?'

'He's fine and newly-shod only two days since. Fretting for some action, though. Where's Newark? Be it a long way off? I never heard on it. This side of Bristol?'

'Much farther, well past the other side, in the east,' Robert told him.

'Fancy that, now. And you'm going to ride that far? Bessy'd better pack you some vittals to keep you from starving on your journey.'

Caroline kept out of his way for the rest of the day, and escaped early to bed, but she could not sleep. She would be losing him so soon, and she had had so little time with him.

After several hours of tossing restlessly, she got up and slipped on her robe. She would go and make herself a posset, one to help her sleep. She crept down the stairs and through into the kitchen. The fire still glowed, and she took a spill and lit a candle, setting it on the table while she found what she needed.

She filled a small pot with water and hung it over the fire to heat while she chopped marjoram and bergamot leaves, and ground some dill seeds.

She poured the water over the herbs and let it steep for a minute, then sat with the tankard in her hands, staring into the embers of the fire, forgetting to drink. Suddenly a noise outside impinged on her thoughts. It was the metallic clang of a horse's shoe on stone, and it was close by.

It was far too late for the villagers to be about. Who could be riding through the village at this time of night?

Afraid, Caroline swiftly blew out the candle and ran through the silent house. She peered from the parlour casement which overlooked the privy garden and beyond it the road. There was no moon, but the sky was clear and the stars bright.

Several men, at least half a dozen, had halted their horses beyond the gate. With painstaking care Caroline eased open the window, holding the catch carefully so that it did not fall back against the window frame. The voice came to her clearly.

'You two round to the back then, and one each to watch the side windows. We know he's here, and we'll have no murderous Royalists escaping the net by jumping out of a window.'

Caroline could hardly breathe. She watched as the men spread out, taking care to make as little noise as possible.

'Seth, you come to the front door with me, but not till the others are in place. We'll count to a hundred, slowly, then I'll move in,' the same voice carried to her.

Caroline pulled the window closed, standing out of sight behind the damask curtain. As soon as it was latched she ran as fast as she could across the room, not even noticing it as her bare toes banged against the end of a heavy settle.

Racing up the stairs she found herself counting, but had only reached ten when she came to the top. She made herself pause to lift the latch of Robert's door as quietly as possible. Then she flung herself across to the bed, dragged the hangings aside and shook him vigorously.

'Robert! Oh, Robert, please, wake up! Quiet, please don't make a noise!'

He had the soldier's ability to wake instantly, and be fully alert. Caroline was still begging him to be silent when he grasped her shoulders and shook her slightly.

'Caroline, calm down! My love, what on earth is it?'

'Listen, I beg of you! And do as I say.

There's no time for argument!' she implored.

'What's frightened you? Let me light a candle, then you can tell me what it is.'

'No! We mustn't show a light. Thank goodness your curtains are drawn, and they won't see our shadows from the firelight, though there isn't much of that.'

'They? Who?'

'Parliament men, at least six of them, surrounding the house and out to catch you,' she gabbled. 'Quickly, get out of bed and pick up your clothes!'

'If they are surrounding the house there is little I can do, dressed or otherwise,' he said calmly.

'But there is!'

She was almost sobbing in her urgency.

'Oh, Robert, don't waste time! Don't argue! I can hide you, but we must be quick.'

To her relief he accepted it, nodded, and swiftly and silently collected his clothes together. She whisked round the room gathering up his other belongings and thrusting them into the saddlebags. She had reason to be thankful both for his neatness, always keeping his possessions in the same places, and the fact she had spent so much time in this room and knew where every item was.

The fireplace was vast, almost as large as the one in the hall beneath, with huge settles built in at either side. Caroline had explained one day that in Tudor times the room had been a parlour where the family could retire in privacy. This had been before the hall was divided to make separate rooms downstairs.

Now she swept the book he'd left on one settle to the floor, twisted a knob in the ornately-carved back, and pulled the seat up to reveal a gaping hole.

'It's a priest's hole. Get in, lie down, and you can wriggle through the back, then work your way round behind the fireplace. I'll throw your clothes and things in after you. Drag them in with you. There's a panel you can slide into place once you're in, so that if they should search it looks an innocent chest. I'll throw in some blankets. That's what we would normally keep in here.'

To her relief he did not argue, but clambered into the settle and lay down as she directed. She went on whispering instructions as he began to crawl through the gap.

'In the little room there's a trap in the floor which leads to a space behind the hall fireplace, and you could get out that way if necessary. I'll let you know when they've gone. Now I must go and warn Jacob.'

He was following her instructions as she spoke, and had no time to say more than a hasty thanks, before she tossed in a couple of blankets from the matching settle, slammed the seat into place and tossed the book back on to it.

Already there was a loud hammering at the front door. She could hear Jacob clumping down the stairs from the attics where the servants slept. He was muttering against heathens who disturbed good folk in their beds at night.

'Jacob!' she hissed, intercepting him outside the bedroom as he went past.

'Mistress Caroline!'

He was scandalised, and Caroline realised that her appearance in the middle of the night, in her nightgown, from Lord Ashring's room, might be interpreted badly. Despite the anxiety she giggled.

'Jacob, it's not what you think. They are Parliament men outside, searching for his lordship. I've hidden him in the priest's hole, and you must not say he is still here.'

To her relief, though he still stared at her, mouth agape, he seemed to understand her words.

'Good fer ye, Mistress Caroline.'

'Say he left early today, and we lent him a horse because his own needed shoeing. Say he was going to Bristol. Let them search if they insist, but make a fuss. Delay them as much as you can.

Now I must warn Bessy and Joan. Oh, and I shall say this is my room, to explain the warm bed. Bessy must come into mine, and we'll say she was unwell. What can it be? I know, her joints pained her and she could not climb all the stairs, so she is sleeping down here for a time. Now go, and play your part well! His lordship's life, and mine, depend on you!'

6

The search was thorough, and the soldiers grew increasingly bad-tempered when no Royalists were found. Jacob dithered. Bessy, hurriedly transferred to Caroline's room, was voluble and indignant. Joan, unusually subdued, forgot to flirt and cowered beneath the covers, emitting squeaks of alarm.

Caroline firmly suppressed her unruly thoughts concerning the strange sensation of being in Robert's bed. She tried to forget she was lying where he had been just minutes earlier, that his warmth enfolded her, and the faint tangy scent of him was all around.

She raised a sleepy tousled head from the pillows, rubbing her eyes, when the soldiers burst into the room. Jacob's protests floated after in after them.

'What — sirs! How dare you enter

my bedchamber?' Caroline demanded, both incredulous and indignant as her bed curtains were swept aside and a lantern thrust near her face.

'You've been harbouring God's enemy!' the leader told her in a sanctimonious tone as he held the lantern aloft and looked suspiciously round the room.

'What on earth do you mean? We're not doing anything of the sort,' she exclaimed.

'Royalist scum!'

He peered behind the window curtains, threw open the lid of a cupboard then turned back towards the bed.

'There are no Royalists here! How dare you make that your paltry excuse for invading my bedchamber!'

Caroline protested vehemently, clutching the bedcovers under her chin.

'His horse is still in the stables! He must be here,' one of the men insisted.

'Oh, him! The stupid fellow who got himself wounded when they tried to steal our horses? I'd have let him die, but Bessy is too soft-hearted and would keep him here until his wound was healed,' she explained, trying desperately to sound convincing.

'You admit it! Where is he?'

'Halfway to Bristol, I should think,' Caroline said coolly, 'if the horse we gave him in exchange for his own isn't lame yet. He didn't know it was prone to throwing a splint. I think we had the better of that bargain. It will repay us for the trouble we had nursing the miserable wretch! And now, I expect an apology from you for bursting so rudely into my bedchamber like this.'

The man in charge glared at her, then suddenly seized the covers and dragged them aside.

'Out. Out of the bed,' he shouted over her now genuinely indignant protests. 'Many a man's been found cowering under his mistress's petticoats.'

As he spoke, he took Caroline's arm and dragged her, furiously berating him, from the bed. He flung her towards the other man, standing grinning in the doorway, and turned to plunge his sword into the mattress.

As Caroline regained her balance, pulled upright by the man who'd caught her, she turned to see a cloud of feathers drift upwards. Then they searched in every possible hiding place, beneath the bed, behind it, on top of the tester, and for good measure between the mattress and the boards.

'He must be here! There's nowhere else.'

'I tell you, he left early this morning. You don't think I would keep a Royalist here longer than I had to? My cousin, who owned this house, fought for Parliament, died fighting the King! I've no love for the Royalists!'

In the end, uttering threats, they had to go. Caroline came down to the hall to make sure the door was locked and barred, then sagged against it with a sigh of relief.

'Oh, Jacob!'

'There, there, Mistress Caroline, they're gone now. You can let his lordship out.'

'Not yet, we must be sure they've really gone,' she said, not prepared to take any risks.

On that thought she moved into the small parlour and peered out of the window. The men were on the far side of the wall, some already on their horses, the rest about to mount.

As Caroline watched, they turned and rode slowly towards the village, out of the valley. She leaned her head against the mullioned glass, suddenly exhausted. Bessy's voice, a piercing whisper, came from the stairs.

'Be they gone, Jacob? Thanks be! I could do with a cup o' my best parsnip wine. Where's Mistress Caroline?'

Caroline went wearily into the hall.

'I'm here, Bessy. I'll go and tell his lordship he can come out now, and we could all do with some wine.'

She climbed the stairs and went back into the bedroom. After looking out through the window, and seeing no trace left of the soldiers, she opened the seat of the settle and called to Robert that he could come out. He struggled out, with some difficulty.

'They must have been very small men, those priests!' he commented, pulling his saddle bags out after him. 'Now what are you laughing at?'

Somehow, in the darkness and the cramped space, he had managed to pull on his shirt and breeches. He was carrying his boots, and his hair was covered in a net of cobwebs, and more hung round him like a ghostly, tattered shroud.

'I'm sorry,' Caroline spluttered. 'You must have terrified all the spiders! We don't sweep and brush in there more than once a century, by the look of you!'

He grinned ruefully, brushing ineffectually at the clinging strands of debris.

'Never mind that, tell me what they knew.'

Caroline sobered, suddenly shivering at the narrowness of their escape. If she hadn't been sleepless and gone to make that posset they'd have all been caught unawares. Then they'd have been dragged off to the nearest lock-up to await trial, no doubt. While she found a brush and helped Robert brush away the worst of the cobwebs, she related what had happened.

'Then I'd best leave straightaway. I can't put you in danger any longer. I can follow the track up on to the moor and make for Barnstaple. Prince Charles and his people will still be there, and I can get news of Rupert.'

Caroline knew there was no choice.

'Bessy is getting some wine. She can pack some food while Jacob gets the horse ready, and you can be away in ten minutes,' she said soberly.

'You're a remarkable girl,' Robert said softly. 'I haven't yet thanked you for your bravery and quick thinking. How did you know they were here?'

'I couldn't sleep, and was down in

the kitchen preparing a tisane. Oh, I never drank it!' she remembered. 'I heard a noise from the outside and went to look out of the parlour window. Then I thought of the hiding place and, well, the rest followed.'

'Have you ever been in it?' he asked, grinning.

'Once, when I was about ten. Peter often played there but I was afraid. I'm sorry you had to hide there.'

'Better to suffer spiders than be strung up on a tree by vengeful rebels. I really am grateful, Caroline, my dear, and one day I'll prove it to you.'

She gazed into his eyes, unable to look away from the dancing gold specks which lit up the dark brown iris. As his hands reached out for her she swayed slowly towards him.

'Mistress Caroline! Be everything all right? My Bessy's got the wine and heated some soup,' came Jacob's voice.

Caroline found herself outside the bedroom door, soothing Jacob and going calmly downstairs. No-one would have guessed the tumult of emotions within her.

Robert had said some day he would thank her properly. What did he mean? Was it a promise for the future, or the meaningless sort of phrase courtiers used?

Confound Jacob for interrupting at that moment. She knew Robert had been about to kiss her, and somehow she also knew that this kiss would have been different from all the others they'd exchanged. It would have meant something, a promise, a commitment, not merely a kiss of gratitude or farewell, the sort she might now receive as he departed from Waring Manor.

Bessy fussed over her, and Robert when he joined them downstairs, and when Caroline eventually asked where Joan was, Bessy snorted in contempt.

'Too much afeard to show her face! Poltroon! She's well to the fore when there's an advantage for her, or she thinks there is, but the first hint of danger and she hides under the bed!

Leave her quaking there.'

They sipped the parsnip wine, potent and sweet. While Bessy found a clean linen napkin and packed food for his lordship, the others tucked into the soup and the remains of a huge apple pie as though they hadn't eaten for days. Then Jacob lit another lantern and went to unbolt the door.

'I'll go and get the horse ready, sir,' he said.

'No, not with a lantern, Jacob. They may have left a man on watch, and we don't want to alert them before I'm ready to ride. Can you manage in the dark or would you prefer I did it? It wouldn't be the first time.'

'I'll do it, sir.'

They were silent for a while after Jacob had gone, and then Robert stood up.

'I'll go and fetch the rest of my things,' he said quietly and left the kitchen.

Bessy, with a sympathetic glance at Caroline, rose and silently began to collect the used bowls and goblets. Caroline took the remains of the food back to the pantry, pausing for a moment to cool her hands on the slate shelf.

She would not weep. Even though she thought her heart must be breaking, she would not allow him to see it when the moment came for Robert to ride out of her life.

During their hurried midnight meal she had convinced herself she would never see him again. His kisses meant nothing, except perhaps gratitude and friendship. His words were empty phrases, and once back with his friends he would forget her.

Caroline realised with a sudden shock that he might even be married. He must be almost thirty years old, high time for a man of his quality to be wed. They had never talked about his home. She did not even know where he might have houses or estates. He could have a wife and several children.

She took a deep breath and walked

firmly back into the kitchen, and relieved her feelings a little by poking the logs on the fire vigorously.

'Don't do that, Mistress Caroline, it'll flare up and burn away before morning,' Bessy remonstrated, but her words were drowned by the sound of an altercation from outside, and both women ran to the door as fast as they could.

'Jacob!' Bessy exclaimed fearfully as the old man was pushed unceremoniously through the doorway.

Caroline looked in astonishment at the man who held Jacob's arms in a fierce grip behind his back.

'John Culham!' she exclaimed. 'What are you doing here in the middle of the night?'

'Where is he? I know he hasn't left. I've had men out watching every track.'

'What do you mean?'

Caroline tried to sound bewildered, but it was becoming clear what had happened. John had called at Waring Manor on his way home, and must have heard about Lord Ashring's presence from the villagers. He was for Parliament — he and Peter had fought together. He must have informed the troop and sent them here! She peered past him but he was apparently alone.

'Why didn't you come with your hired bullies?' she demanded hotly. 'Were you too ashamed, informing on me? And you a friend of Peter's! Those ill-mannered louts dragged me unceremoniously out of bed. Did they tell you that?'

He grinned triumphantly.

'They did, and wished they'd had more time to dally with you, they said. But I found it very strange you should be sleeping in Peter's old room!'

'Our sleeping arrangements are none of your business!' Caroline snapped. 'But your men found no-one here. All we did was look after a man I wounded accidentally. Nothing but common charity, if you know what that is. And he left this morning.'

'Without his horse? You can't trick

me, Caroline. You hadn't a horse in the stables that a soldier would have looked at twice, while that great brute Jacob was getting ready in secret just now stood idle.'

'The horse had a colic. I were but seein' he was comfortable, as I was up anyway,' Jacob intervened.

'Believe what you like,' Caroline said contemptuously, turning away, 'but leave us in peace. We've been disturbed enough tonight and I want to go back to bed.'

'To act as watchdog over the priest's hole?' he asked softly. 'Did you forget Peter and I used to play there as boys? I know all about it. Well, my men will be back in a few minutes, and then we'll flush out your precious cavalier!'

7

You shall not!' Caroline declared. 'I'm in charge here, for young James. I will not permit you to search the house!'

'You cannot stop me,' he replied calmly.

He paused consideringly, then smiled ruefully.

'Caroline, we were friends once. I was with Peter, and I know how much he loved you. Surely you believe in the same things he did. The right of men to have a say in Parliament, to disagree with the King when he is wrong, to set their own taxation for their own needs, not just for spending on vainglorious adventures in Europe, fighting other rulers' battles.'

'I know nothing of politics,' Caroline said cautiously. 'I never did, but I don't see why there has to be so much killing.'

She would have supported Peter's views unthinkingly once, but since Robert had talked with her and explained his own reasons for supporting the King, she'd become uncertain. There were arguments on both sides, and she favoured neither one nor the other.

'But you must have heard the King's cause is all but finished?' John said.

'No, we don't get a great deal of news here in the valley, and we never know what to believe anyway,' Caroline retorted sharply. 'It seems to depend on who is doing the telling.'

'The King's strongholds are falling. He has almost no supporters left apart from here in Devon and Cornwall, and with Fairfax and Cromwell approaching they won't last out for long,' John said persuasively.

'Then why should it matter whether one Royalist escapes the net? It can't be very important.'

Caroline shrugged her shoulders,

trying to look petulant, as she faced up to Culham.

'All men who cause such trouble are to be tried and punished as they deserve.'

'That could apply to either side,' she said crossly.

She was praying that Robert would not walk unaware into the kitchen. Let him realise, and retreat once more into the priest's room. Culham cast her an impatient glance.

'This particular Royalist is more than a mere troublemaker,' he explained with exaggerated patience. 'He is dangerous, if he manages to get through to the King. We know he has been recently to Ireland, and has news of what foreign support the King may expect. The Queen and others are busy spreading false rumours around the European Courts, and this man knows exactly to what effect. We need to know what support might come for the King in order to prepare suitable defences.'

'I told you, he left early today,'

Caroline lied again, trying to put as much conviction into her voice as possible.

'I don't believe you. I think you're seeking to protect him. He has bewitched you, made you think he loves you, no doubt, and trapped you into working for the King.'

'That's utter nonsense!' Caroline's voice said, while her mind knew that he was correct in that she loved Robert.

She did not work for the King, however, and never would. How could a mere girl do that, she wondered irrelevantly. But how did he know? As if she had spoken aloud John Culham ignored her denial, and went on slowly.

'We have our supporters in every village, you know,' he said menacingly.

'Spies,' she interrupted contemptuously.

'Whatever the squires believe, men think for themselves. Peter took a few of the younger tenants or their sons with him, and they died with him, too. Their fathers and brothers have no love for the King. They've seen you and this man dallying on the moor, hand in hand, and no doubt more intimate embraces have been exchanged when you've been more secluded.'

'How dare you insinuate such things!'

Caroline tried to cover her dismay with anger. There was anger that people she had believed to be loyal tenants or friends had spied on her and Robert.

But there was also anger at themselves, that they had not been more discreet. Most of all she was furious that it was true. They had only their own carelessness to blame.

Whatever her own feelings she still could not quite believe it meant nothing to Robert, though it would have been natural enough, she thought bleakly, for a man to while away an idle week or so with dalliance.

'I dare to say the truth,' John went on. 'But if he's still here, Caroline, and you'll endeavour to find out from him what we want to know, that would be more valuable to us than he would be himself. He'd not reveal his knowledge to us though we tore out his nails and threatened him with a traitor's death.'

'You would torture him?'

She was aghast.

'No more than he deserves. Will you not help us, for the sake of Peter's memory?'

'It would be a sad memorial to an honourable man to make me a spy!' Caroline retorted furiously.

'Hardly spying. Ashring's a traitor who seeks to bring foreign armies on to English soil. That would lead to more fighting, more deaths. Would you not work to prevent that?'

'I want nothing to do with either side, and I could hardly spy on a man who is presently riding towards Bristol.'

'He has you even more in thrall than I imagined. Then I've no alternative. I must search the house.'

'You shall not! If my word is not good enough, I am sorry for our former friendship, but I will not permit another search.'

'You cannot prevent it. I have the right, and enough men to enforce it. But first, you must all go into the cellar.'

'The cellar?'

Caroline's voice rose in astonishment.

'I regret, but I cannot permit you to hamper us. My men are outside, awaiting my signal, and that pernicious Royalist will not escape us this time. If I hadn't been delayed before, they'd have known about the secret room and Ashring would have been on his way by now, in chains.'

Caroline went slowly towards him. She was only a girl, and Bessy and Jacob were old, but surely between them they could overpower John Culham for long enough to permit Robert to leave. It was his only chance now. Since John Culham knew about the hiding place, it was no longer of value.

Culham guessed her intention, however, and gave a harsh laugh as he stepped back. When Jacob moved forwards he pushed the old man viciously aside so that he stumbled and collapsed on to the bench by the table.

'Not that way, little Caroline,' John said brutally, grinning at her with evil in his eyes.

He whipped out his sword, stepping forward and pressing the point into her breast.

He glanced across at Bessy, who had rushed to help Jacob, and was now staring at him, her hands to her mouth.

'Open the cellar door and bring me the key. Then get yourself and the old fool down there. Move! Every second you delay makes it more likely little Caroline here will be hurt!'

'Typical of Cromwell's bullies, to attack women, like they did after Naseby,' a calm, quiet voice interrupted.

Caroline, heedless of the sword held to her heart, swung round with a gasp of dismay. Surely he would not meekly give himself up! He mustn't be allowed to do it!

'Robert!' she exclaimed, and took a hasty step towards him, her hands held out in supplication.

Lord Ashring stood in the doorway leading from the hall. He had his own sword raised, and there was a grim, determined smile on his handsome face.

'Out of the way, Caroline. I'll deal with this scum who can only fight women!'

On the words, he advanced slowly into the room, and Caroline was brushed aside as Culham turned to face him. Bessy grasped her hand when she seemed inclined to move towards his lordship, and pulled her across to the nook beside the fire where Jacob was already huddling, nursing his bruised arms and wrists, sore from Culham's callous mistreatment.

'Leave it to his lordship, Miss Caroline!' she begged urgently. 'He'll show that devil how to treat honest folk!'

There were two lanterns alight on the table in the centre of the room, and the fire which Caroline had poked was beginning to flare, casting enormous shadows on the far wall.

Caroline's gaze was fixed unmovingly on Robert. He wore just his shirt, open at the neck and tucked firmly into tight fitting breeches, and was in stockinged feet.

This, she soon realised, gave him an advantage over John Culham, encumbered with a heavy riding coat and boots. He could move with greater speed over the stone-flagged floor, while Culham more than once found his feet slipping on the smooth stone and had to pause to regain his balance.

For some time they circled one another warily, testing each other's skills, then Robert suddenly increased the pressure, moving forward decisively, pressing hard and forcing Culham back with a rapid flurry of slashes and lunges. If Culham had not moved quickly to put the table between himself and Robert the end would have come very swiftly.

The table provided a respite for him and for a while they circled it warily, but it was large and Robert was unable to get within striking distance.

Then Culham suddenly moved backwards towards the group in the chimney corner and reached for Caroline's hand. He dragged her towards him and twisted her in front of him, clamped rigidly to his body. He had a dagger in his left hand, and its point was a bare inch from her throat.

'Come nearer and I'll make sure you don't enjoy the pretty little wench's favours again,' he sneered, beginning to drag Caroline towards the outer door.

She resisted fiercely, kicking his shins and trying to bite the hand which held the dagger, heedless of whether it scratched her or not, but he was far too strong. Her mind worked even faster than when she had been inventing the story to tell the soldiers.

She knew the door was shut and he

would need to use one hand to lift the latch. This would have to be his right hand if he wished to keep her imprisoned.

The second she saw the sword move backwards as he felt for the latch, she threw herself to that side, and as she fell thrust her foot between Culham's ankles.

He was thrown off balance as he tried to restrain her, and within seconds Robert was once more threatening him. If Caroline had not been lying between them, impeding Robert's movements as well as Culham's, it would have finished then. But somehow Culham scrambled away. Once more the devilish shadow-dance began.

Caroline rose cautiously to her feet and put a hand to her cheek. The dagger had slid across it and there was a trace of sticky blood on her face, but the cut was slight. Even more determined to help Robert now, she darted towards the table. It had saved Culham before, and if she could move it back,

Robert would have greater space. Culham would have nowhere to retreat.

It was far too heavy, but the bench was not. She dragged it out to make a barrier over which Culham would have to climb if he tried once more to put the table between them, or over which he might fall and strike his head, she thought hopefully. For a moment she marvelled at the bloodthirsty nature she was revealing.

Culham had seen her manoeuvre and kept away from the table. Within minutes, Robert, who despite his illness was by far the better swordsman, had driven Culham cunningly into a corner. A few more moves, a feint, a lunge, and suddenly, as Robert twisted his sword aside, his adversary's weapon was spinning away from him through the air.

'Drop the dagger,' Robert said calmly, only slightly out of breath.

Culham was breathing more deeply, sucking air desperately into his lungs.

'You'll not get away, you devil! My

men are waiting!' he gasped. 'They'll soon capture you.'

'Kill the pesky rebel!' Jacob quavered.

Robert smiled slightly.

'I think it will be enough to tie him up and leave him somewhere — the priest's hole, perhaps?'

'You couldn't!' Culham's voice was weak. 'They'd never find me there! I'd be dead within hours!'

'No, unfortunately, that I could not do. I've no wish to have your wretched life on my conscience. The cellar will do. Caroline, have you some strong rope?'

'I'll get some,' Jacob offered, sounding disappointed.

Then, to Culham's obvious dismay, he stood guard with both daggers while Lord Ashring tied Culham's hands and feet and pushed him into the cellar.

'What in the world shall we do now?' Bessy asked tearfully. 'They'll take Mistress Caroline when they come, and heaven knows what they'll do to her.'

Jacob was entering into the realms of

conspiracy with considerable gusto. He was chortling with glee as he made his suggestion, cleverly thought out.

'Lock us all into one of the attic bedrooms, and then we can say we had to do what you said, you'd threatened us if we dain't. We'll be safe enough.'

'But if they didn't come, you'd none of you be able to get out,' Robert said, highly amused despite the predicament they found themselves in.

'Don't you fret. I can open they pesky little locks,' Jacob said contemptuously.

'Even if they let us go they'd still blame Mistress Caroline,' Bessy said gloomily. 'They wouldn't believe she was innocent, not with Mr Culham to say how she helped you.'

'Caroline must come with me and I will escort her to her uncle at Falmouth.'

8

Caroline knew her only hope of safety was to go with Robert. That she also wanted to made her impatient when Bessy began to protest it wasn't right, a young girl going off alone with a man.

'Bessy, they'll make me a prisoner if I don't! Would you prefer that? And worse? You heard from John Culham what those others said about me.'

'Go and pack saddlebags with the minimum you can take,' Robert said briskly. 'Jacob, saddle mine and the best horse you have for her, and muffle their hooves in straw and rags. We'll lead them on to the moor and hope the soldiers lose us.'

'Put Peter's saddle on Jacob,' Caroline said suddenly. 'I'll wear his old clothes and ride as a boy. It will be safer.'

She ran out of the kitchen and as

soon as he saw Jacob obeying his commands, Robert followed. A few minutes later he was back fully dressed, packing into his own saddlebags the packets of food Bessy had hastily prepared.

Caroline came down a little self consciously. She felt surprisingly naked without her petticoats. She had on a pair of worn breeches which Peter had discarded many years since. They were still too large for her, and she'd tied them with a length of cord. With them she wore a white shirt with hastily-tied cravat, and a thick, homespun riding coat.

She had considered cutting her hair, but hadn't time to make a tidy job of it, so had stuffed it beneath a wide-brimmed hat, somewhat bedraggled. A jaunty feather drooping over her right eye made her look decidedly rakish.

Peter's shoes had all been too large, but her own riding boots did not look too odd. She'd slipped a dagger into the top of one, feeling foolish but defiant.

She needed a weapon of some sort.

Robert nodded approvingly and picked up his saddlebags.

'Good, come quickly and make as little sound as you can,' he said hastily.

There was no time for more than a quick hug from Bessy, who was sniffing ominously, and still muttering that it wasn't seemly, before Robert led the way to the stables. Jacob had a small lantern alight there, with just one side open giving him a faint glow by which to work.

He blinked a little and raised an eyebrow when he saw Caroline's attire, but said nothing while he arranged the saddlebags on the two horses standing in readiness.

'I've put the pistols in holsters, Mistress Caroline, and they're primed and ready to fire,' Jacob whispered conspiratorially as he turned back to her.

'Just aim well away from me,' Robert commented wryly. 'Though on second thoughts, perhaps you'd best aim at me, then I'll be safe,' he added, grinning.

How could he joke when his life was in danger? Caroline, who'd been too busy for anything but the most immediate planning, felt her spirits suddenly soar. With such a man she'd be safe. He'd never allow harm to come to them.

Within minutes they were cautiously leading the horses through the fields, avoiding the track towards the moors in case Culham's men were waiting. Both of them had a hand ready to stifle any betraying whinny if their mounts caught the scent of other horses.

They reached the open moor safely, and when Robert judged they were well out of reach he stopped and hitched the reins to the branch of a lone tree.

'We'll ride now. Can you take the rags from his hooves?'

'Yes.'

Caroline bent to the task.

'Oughtn't you really to be going to find the king, as John Culham said?'

'Tyler took my letters. The rest can

wait. I'll go first to Prince Charles at Barnstaple, and discover what's been happening.'

'But you cannot escort me all the way to Falmouth. It would waste too much precious time. If you've news for the King why can't I come with you?'

'You'd be going through enemy-held country, and I'm not inconsiderate enough to leave you alone and unprotected, Caroline! My news is far from good, and the King will almost certainly have heard by now. I'm much later than I intended, remember.'

Caroline blushed. That was her fault.

'Did it — would it have made much difference?' she asked in a subdued voice.

'No, my sweet. Don't blame yourself. Neither France nor Spain can afford men to help, and will merely be sending embassies to England. Some form of negotiation is the only way Charles can now keep his throne.'

They mounted and set off. They had to go cautiously in the dark, for the track was poor and there were sudden dips into hidden hollows, boulders to avoid, and streams swollen with the recent rains. By dawn they were still some miles short of Barnstaple.

'We must stay up on the moor and hide during the day,' Robert decided. 'It would be foolhardy to ride into Barnstaple unless we know it is still safe in Royalist hands. If the rebels could ride unhindered as far as Waring Manor they might be farther into Devon than we thought. And we both of us need to rest. We can find a secure spot and sleep for a while.'

They found a tiny secluded valley, watered by a stream, with a dense thicket of trees and undergrowth where they and the horses could remain hidden. They took the horses to drink, then hobbled them amongst the trees where there was a fortuitous clearing with sweet grass for them to nibble. Robert unstrapped the saddle-bags and arranged them as pillows, softened by two blankets Jacob had strapped on behind.

'First we must eat, to keep up our strength, then you will try to sleep while I keep watch.'

'But you must be as tired as I am,' Caroline protested. 'Surely we're safe here.'

'We are never safe anywhere,' he replied soberly. 'Later I'll sleep for an hour or so while you keep guard.'

As she tucked into Bessy's pie Caroline felt a wave of exhaustion sweep over her. Within minutes she was asleep, curled up on the ground but oblivious of its hardness.

Robert gazed down at her. She still looked a child, yet she'd been so valiant in protecting first her home and then him. He covered her with his cloak and sat with his back against the trunk of a tree.

As a soldier he was used to going without food and sleep, but his head was aching. His wound still troubled him occasionally, and he knew he was not entirely fit. He must regain his full strength before the decisive battle came.

★ ★ ★

Caroline awoke as the pale, wintry sun reached its height. She was stiff, and for a moment disorientated. Where was she? Why was she asleep in the open, the sky above her, trees all around? Recollection swept back in a flash. She looked for Robert, to find him smiling kindly down at her.

'Time to eat again, then I can snatch a few hours,' he said, helping her to sit up.

'I don't think I'm hungry,' she said slowly.

'You'll still eat. We may not have another chance today. We must set out the moment it's dark.'

Meekly she obeyed, and afterwards he rolled himself in the cloak and slept. Caroline feasted her eyes on his beloved face. She knew every line of those high, slanting cheekbones, thin nose, and exciting, tantalising lips. She realised with a slight shock that while she had been asleep he had somehow shaved.

How many men, she wondered, on the run from deadly enemies, and no doubt exhausted, would have bothered to shave off their stubble with no more than cold water from a stream?

His fastidiousness, which had impressed her earlier, now made her love him even more fiercely. She vowed that even if she had to give her life to prevent it, he would not be allowed to fall into the hands of the Roundheads. No such sacrifice was called for, however. They resumed their journey at dusk, and despite having to travel cautiously, reached Barnstaple before dawn.

'I think it best if I take a private room at an inn,' Robert said as they crossed the long stone bridge. 'Then you can sleep while I go and see the Prince's friends.'

Caroline was reluctant to part from him, but she was suddenly shy of being seen in her boy's raiment, so she made no protest. When he had seen her safely into a small room under the eaves, the best that could be provided, Robert kissed her briefly and bade her let no-one into the room but himself.

She sank down on to the bed, her hand touching her brow where his lips had rested so briefly. Did he feel anything for her or was she but a nuisance, delaying him from his real concerns? Had the kiss been one of comfort, given unthinkingly? It was very different from those they'd exchanged earlier.

She was soon asleep, exhausted and stiff from the unaccustomed long hours in the saddle, and the short sleep on hard ground the previous day.

When she awoke she knew instantly there was someone else in the room, and looked about her cautiously. Yes, there was steady breathing. Slowly she raised her head, and with a gasp of relief saw Robert stretched out on the floor near the door, his head pillowed on one of the saddlebags.

Her movement roused him and he sat up instantly, then grinned at her mischievously.

'You looked so peaceful, as if you hadn't a care in the world,' he said, smiling in a way that made her heart turn over with love. 'I couldn't bear to wake you.'

'You must be tired. What o'clock is it? And did you see the Prince of Wales?'

'Midday, just after. Are you hungry? Dinner will be ready soon, but I brought bread and cheese, ale and some apples in with me. Eat, while I tell you the news.'

She ate ravenously, and when she was sitting cross-legged on the bed, chewing an apple, while Robert sat beside her, he told her what he'd discovered.

'The King is at Newark. He seems to be making for Scotland. But otherwise it is all disaster.'

'Robert!'

She held out her hand and tentatively, for his face was forbidding at the memory, she touched his shoulder. Suddenly he turned towards her and clasped her to him, while she pushed off his hat and gently stroked his dark, springing curls.

'The King refused to believe Rupert acted to save as many men as possible at Bristol,' he said slowly. 'Rupert is with him now, but reports say Digby is still in the ascendant, has in fact been given much of Rupert's command and sent North to try and join Montrose. If Scotland is safe, no doubt the King will go there. Most of his other garrisons, Chester, Winchester, as well as most in Wales, and even Basing House, have fallen. Fairfax has captured Tiverton.'

'Tiverton?' Caroline exclaimed. 'Just the far side of Exmoor? Then that explains why John Culham and his men were so close to Waring Manor. But is the Prince of Wales safe here?'

'No, he's left Barnstaple to go westwards.'

'Then what will you do?' Caroline asked gently. 'Do you not want to join Prince Rupert and the King?'

'I will take you to Falmouth,' he said briskly, the moment of weakness past. 'There seems no point in trying to reach the King. One more man will make little difference. And from what they say he already has too many officers and too few ordinary soldiers at Newark!' he added wryly.

'You can follow the Prince of Wales. He'll be going into Cornwall. Is it safe for him?'

'For the moment. There have for long been arguments about where he should go if England becomes unsafe. I can best serve him by offering my knowledge of what is happening in the countries I have visited.'

'Do we start today, riding tonight again?' Caroline asked.

Suddenly she was cold, knowing their time together was very short. He grinned, his spirits restored, and stood up.

'No, you shall have a night at least in a comfortable bed, my love, and we can ride safely through the day. The rebels are not yet in control here.'

9

'If you insist on such ridiculous gallantry, and are stupid enough to sleep on the floor, then I will, too!' Caroline declared heatedly.

'My dear Caroline, can you not see the invidious position we are already in, sharing a room, without sharing a bed, too?' Robert asked wearily.

The argument had raged for half an hour.

'There's no-one to see what we do.' Caroline stormed. 'You're not well, your head pains you. I can tell from the way you frown at me, it's not all bad temper!' she added bluntly.

Suddenly he laughed.

'Do you ever give up?'

'Not when I know I'm in the right. Robert, the bed is wide, you can sleep fully-clothed if you will, and with a bolster between us, or on top of the covers if you choose to freeze. But you will not sleep on hard boards while there is a soft, and unusually clean, feather mattress available.'

'Very well, I surrender to a woman,' he said resignedly. 'I will go to the taproom while you prepare for bed.'

Before she could reply he left the room and Caroline stared after him. Now she was in a dilemma. She had packed no nightgown in the haste of departure, and considered her shirt alone would be too indecorous. She must retain her breeches. Within five minutes she was in bed, shivering slightly although it was not cold, huddled under the covers with her face turned ostentatiously away from the other half.

It was less roomy than she'd imagined, she discovered. She eased over to the edge, and hoped Robert would be comfortable on the portion which remained.

When the door opened she closed her eyes determinedly and tried to breathe slowly and evenly. After what seemed an inordinate length of time the candle was blown out, a lifted blanket let in a draught of colder air, the bed creaked, and she could feel Robert carefully disposing his long limbs beside her.

Eventually she fell into a doze and it was dawn before she woke. Recalling instantly where she was, she opened her eyes. In confused dismay she discovered that during the night she had turned to face Robert. She'd somehow rolled towards him, and he'd gathered her into his arms.

She dared not move in case she disturbed him. He would be as aghast as she was to discover how they'd slept. She could only hope he would move and release her before he woke.

It seemed hours to Caroline, hours during which she swung from the extremes of embarrassment at the position she was in, and delight at being so closely embraced by her beloved Robert, even though it was unintentional and he had no know-ledge of it.

The thought crossed her mind once that he might be imagining she was someone else, but she pushed it away hastily. She'd never asked him about his private life, and she refused to think about the possibility of other women in it.

When she was growing cramped with the effort of keeping still he suddenly stirred, stretched both arms up, and she was able to slide hurriedly out of the bed.

'Good morning, my lord. I trust you slept well,' she said in a stiff, curt tone.

'Indeed I did. I slept better than I've done for months,' he said contentedly. 'And you? I hope I didn't disturb you too much. The bed wasn't as wide as perhaps you thought.'

'Wide enough,' Caroline said sharply, trying to ignore his glinting smile. 'Which way do we travel today?'

'So eager to leave? We would do best to keep on the north coast, I think, to avoid Dartmoor. Once past it we shall no doubt discover where the Prince is and be able to join him for a while before we go to Falmouth.'

They did follow the coast road for two days, sleeping the first in a small inn with no other guests, so that Robert was able to hire two rooms.

The following evening they came to the small town, no more than a village, where the entourage of the young Prince of Wales had taken up temporary residence. The Prince and his more important advisers were in the largest inn, while others found accommodation as best they could in a smaller inn and the houses of villagers.

Caroline had to wait in the taproom while Robert was closeted with the Prince upstairs. She endured the curious stares of idle courtiers as stoically as possible, pretending intense interest in the small grey stone cottages on the other side of the main street.

When Robert returned he indicated they should go outside before he spoke.

He led the way along a narrow, twisting lane, which climbed a steep hill towards small, bare fields.

'Is it so very bad?' Caroline asked in the end, when he made no effort to speak.

'They are all, it seems, bent upon wantonly destroying the cause. The King appears to have turned completely against Rupert,' he replied grimly. 'Then Rupert himself, perhaps naturally after all the argument, rebels!'

'Rebels? How? What happened?'

'Rupert is the one man who's worked unceasingly to keep the King on his throne, the only competent leader amongst that pack of self-seeking, squabbling rabble! Perhaps the King despairs, turns to others when the situation is hopeless, but it will not serve!'

'What has he done?' she prompted urgently when he paused yet again.

He sighed wearily.

'The latest news is that Rupert demanded a council of war should hear his reasons for surrendering Bristol, and they accepted them as justified. But the King does not. He then proposed removing Willis, who is Governor of Newark and one of Rupert's friends, to a lesser post in Oxford. When Willis and Rupert and Prince Maurice protested, the King called it mutiny and sent them away from Newark. He's few enough friends left, Caroline. Must he dismiss the truest of them?' he asked in anguish.

There was little Caroline could do to comfort him. She walked beside him, climbing up the steep lane which wound and twisted its way amongst stone cottages.

When they had almost reached the end and only a couple of cottages remained before the open fields, she ventured to speak.

'Where are we going?' she asked quietly, and Robert turned towards her with a rueful smile.

'Caroline, my dear, I'm sorry. I forgot to tell you. I've arranged for you to stay with one of the ladies, Mistress Julia Somerton, and her husband.'

'You're leaving me?' Caroline exclaimed in dismay.

It had come, and she discovered that she wasn't prepared.

'Only for a while, until we travel to Falmouth. I must stay here a few days. There are matters to discuss, and it would not do for us to be together. You must see that.'

Caroline did see. He wished to separate himself from her. In the depths of her mind she knew his reasons were sensible ones, but all she could think of was that after these precious few days of his company she was to lose him.

'Am I to remain a boy?' she asked lightly.

'Julia knows the truth, but it is as you wish.'

She did not reply, and giving her a brief smile he turned towards the last cottage, a small, square building with the door opening directly on to the stony path.

Julia Somerton was a tall, pale, elegant beauty. She smiled warmly at Robert, and gave Caroline an unsmiling nod which indicated she knew she was there but had no welcome attached.

'My poor Robert! What a dreadful misfortune for you! You come through battles unscathed, and then Edward says you were accidentally shot by some country yokel. Such clods ought not to be allowed to handle weapons!'

Caroline gasped, but Robert touched her arm warningly and she bit back the retort on her tongue. Perhaps he would not wish this supercilious, young woman to know that it was a girl who had injured him. The thought increased the guilt she still felt, and she was unusually subdued as Robert explained he was escorting Caroline to Falmouth but needed to remain here a day or so for discussions with the Prince's men.

'I will come back to see you in the morning, Caroline,' he said, and left abruptly.

Julia regarded Caroline in some amusement.

'Poor Robert,' she murmured. 'He's too willing to shoulder the burdens of others. But only to a limited extent. He will not sacrifice his entire future.'

'What do you mean?' Caroline asked warily.

'You haven't a hope of entrapping him into marriage,' Julia said calmly, a smile of amusement playing over her lips.

'Why should you think I wish to?' Caroline demanded angrily.

She'd never dared hope for that.

'My dear, it's obvious by the look in your eyes. You cannot bear him out of your sight.'

'I've never thought of the possibility,' Caroline retorted, and inside herself marvelled that it was, strangely, true.

All she'd dreamed of was being with Robert for ever. How it was to be achieved hadn't once occurred to her. Julia laughed in disbelief, however.

'I'm no fool, and Robert is a very

attractive man. If I didn't have my Edward I'd be making a play for him myself,' she continued musingly, and Caroline knew instinctively that Edward was no barrier.

If Julia wanted Robert she would ignore her husband.

'He merely offered to escort me to Falmouth, where some members of my family are living,' she said stiffly. 'I could not remain at home after helping him escape the Roundheads. He feels an obligation towards me, that's all.'

'I'm sure it is, on his part! But you're hoping for more. Don't bother to deny it. Is it the reason for this ridiculous masquerade in male clothing? Do you think you're more desirable in breeches?'

'I don't think it necessary to analyse me, mistress, as if I were a horse for sale!'

Caroline by now was furiously angry, and although the woman was her hostess she felt no obligation to observe normal politeness. Julia had been the first to abandon the courtesies, after all.

'Robert is a wealthy man, as well as an attractive one,' the insidious voice went on. 'His mother was French, and a very rich heiress, so even if the King loses his throne and we all have to flee abroad, Robert will lose little. He won't have lost all for a stupid sense of honour, and be begging his crusts in Europe like the rest of us!' she added rather bitterly, Caroline observed.

'I'm well aware that Robert regards me as no more than someone he offered to help,' Caroline stated as calmly as she could under the circumstances. 'It grows late and I am tired. Could you tell me, please, where I'm to sleep?'

'What a pity for you that you cannot sleep in Robert's arms tonight.'

Julia laughed softly.

'Is that why you donned male clothing, in the hope that you could share inn rooms without arousing comment?'

She laughed again as Caroline's face flamed.

'You are in the wrong,' Caroline said as calmly as she could. 'If I may go to my room.'

'Your room is the one on the right at the top of the stairs,' Julia said sweetly. 'Even if Robert felt an obligation, he is betrothed to the daughter of a French duke. He wouldn't desert her for a little nobody who cavorts in breeches.'

10

For two days Caroline avoided the gloating Julia Somerton by going for long, solitary walks on the beach or through the bleak upland fields. She also avoided Robert, who had sent messages apologising for the delay to their journey.

She'd no wish to see him again, and on the first morning spent several hours debating with herself, trying to decide what to do. It was not his fault, she reminded herself continually, that she had fallen in love with him. His kisses and embraces meant nothing to him, whatever their effect on her.

Could she ride to Falmouth alone? Much as she was tempted, it would take her at least two days and she had no money to pay for lodging at an inn. It had not occurred to her to bring money during that hurried packing. In any event, they'd used very little money at Waring Manor. They produced most of what was needed in the village, buying a few things from travelling peddlers. They never kept large amounts of money in the house.

She would have slept under a hedge in summer, but she knew it would be foolhardy at the beginning of November. Dared she take the chance of finding a barn?

At this point in her reflections she lifted her chin defiantly. Why should she pay heed to this woman? To run away would be an admission that Julia's remarks had hurt. She would not give the woman the satisfaction of knowing how right she'd been, at least in her suspicion that Caroline was in love with Robert.

She still kept out of Julia's way, however, returning to the cottage only in time for dinner. Afterwards she sat in the tiny bedroom repairing some tears in Peter's ancient riding coat.

★ ★ ★

On the third day, at dawn, before Caroline was fully dressed, Robert appeared at the cottage. She dragged on her shoes and the hat which covered her hair, and ran down the stairs.

'We should leave at once,' he said briskly, giving her no other greeting. 'Are you ready?'

'I'll get the saddlebags,' Caroline replied, equally abrupt. 'Where are the horses?'

'At the top of the lane. We can take a track through the fields. It serves as a short cut.'

They rode in silence for some time, then Robert seemed to throw off his offhand attitude and turned towards her.

'My apologies, Caroline. It's been a difficult couple of days for me. Did Julia entertain you well? She's probably as bored as the other wives, waiting there and not knowing how long they'll remain, or where they'll be going next.'

'I don't think Mistress Somerton was bored,' Caroline said briefly, but tactfully decided to say no more about the lady's comments to her while she was her guest at the cottage. 'Do you expect to reach Falmouth tomorrow?'

'That is the plan, if all goes well. Did Julia tell you much of what is happening?'

'No.'

Caroline did not elaborate.

'The Prince is receiving a bombardment of instructions, from the King, from his mother in France, and from everyone else, about where he should go,' he said with a sigh. 'It's always been agreed he must not fall into the hands of Parliament, for that would put unbearable pressure on the King. But no-one can agree in whose hands he would be the safest.'

'Where does the King himself wish him to go?' Caroline asked, intrigued.

'He cannot make up his mind, which is the major difficulty. He is swayed almost daily, by events or by the counsel of those who have seen him last.'

'It does not seem very kingly,' Caroline commented.

She was beginning to wonder whether this King, with his uncertainties and his lack of loyalty to friends such as Prince Rupert, was a man worth fighting for.

Robert echoed her thoughts.

'No, but being a king does not ensure wisdom,' Robert said with a shrug. 'If Charles had been wiser there might not have been war, and if he'd listened more to men like Rupert it might have been conducted differently. All we can do now, since the war would appear to be lost, is to prepare for the future, for Prince Charles.'

'What will happen to the King?' she asked, alarmed.

Whatever his faults she didn't wish him any harm.

'Who can say? But he'll never again be permitted to rule unfettered. Parliament will always be stronger now. Some think he'll be fortunate to retain his throne.'

This was such a tremendous calamity Caroline was silent for several miles. They'd always had a King. It was impossible to imagine life without a King on the throne.

What could they do instead? Would Parliament rule? More importantly, what would Robert be doing? At last she could bear the suspense no longer.

'What do you intend to do after we reach Falmouth?' she asked quietly. 'Will you go to France?'

'Yes. I have estates there, and can help prepare the way if the Prince is eventually sent to France.'

He seemed about to say more but stopped, and instead began to point out various features of the countryside. They paused at noon to eat some of the food he had brought, but their conversation was stilted and spasmodic.

'Where do you expect to spend tonight?' Caroline asked as the pale, wintry sun fell over the horizon in front of them.

'I'd hoped we might reach St Columb. We're north of Bodmin now, but could stop there if you're weary.'

'I'd prefer to get as far as possible, to reach Falmouth earlier,' Caroline said quickly, avoiding his eyes.

'As you wish. Tell me about your uncle.'

'There isn't much to say. He is Peter's uncle, actually, not mine. He does not like the country, and has a house in Falmouth where he spends all his time. I believe he has a share in a trading ship. His wife comes from the area and they have three sons. The middle one is the same age as James, which was fortunate, as he lives with them and has companionship.'

'Do you like him?'

'I'm not related to him. He was displeased, I think, when Peter and I were betrothed. His wife had a niece whose fortune was greater than mine, and he wished Peter to marry her.'

'Then it seems as though you don't relish throwing yourself on his mercy?'

'There's no alternative. At least he will provide me with a home until he can marry me off. The local innkeeper or ship's chandler will be considered suitable matches, no doubt,' she could not resist adding, her tone bitter.

How different to the life she'd once looked forward to as Sir Peter Waring's wife! But here she firmly suppressed her thoughts. She hadn't imagined the possibility of marriage with Robert until the wretched Julia had thrown scorn on the idea.

'Caroline!'

She turned towards him, surprised at the change in tone.

'What is it?' she asked, startled.

'Caroline, there is something I have been meaning to say to you, to ask. But there has been so much else for me to think of, so many distractions and there's never seemed to be a suitable time, and this is possibly not — '

He paused, and in the silence a shot rang out, stark and sudden in the still evening. Caroline's horse, normally well-mannered, placid, reared up in fright. She managed to retain her seat with a somewhat undignified clutch at his mane, but was unable to prevent him from bolting.

As she clung desperately to the saddle and they raced along the track she could hear more hooves thundering along behind her. Feeling more secure, she risked a glance back and found Robert pounding in her wake.

'Keep going!' he shouted, and she nodded, urging her horse on instead of trying to slow him.

The track widened and Robert brought his own more powerful beast alongside.

'Bandits or highwaymen,' he shouted across to her. 'Not soldiers, this far West.'

That was little consolation, she thought wryly. They still had guns. She looked back over her shoulder. A pair of men behind were keeping pace with them.

'The pistols, that Jacob put in for you. Can you give me one?' Robert asked.

'Yes.'

Caroline's horse by now was flagging, and she was able to draw the pistol carefully out of the holster. It took some moments to twist it round, she was so afraid of dropping it, but eventually she held it out for Robert. He reached over precariously and took it from her with a brief word of thanks.

'Keep riding, and you'll come to an inn soon. Less than a mile, I think. I'll follow when I've dealt with them,' he ordered.

On the last words, he slowed his horse and with a skill Caroline envied, he twisted the animal round so that within a yard he was facing the other way, and the pistol had been aimed and fired. Caroline, unwilling to leave him, despite his commands, had managed to bring her own tired beast to a stop a few yards farther on, and she turned in the saddle to see what was happening. Would they shoot again? Had they another gun?

Then a sound in front alerted her and she realised with dismay that two more riders were approaching from the opposite direction. From the encouraging shouts they must be more robbers. It had been a trap. Behind, one of the robbers had been shot and his horse, terrified, could be heard plunging away across the open moor. Robert had his own pistols out now and as Caroline watched he fired again, felling the second man of the pair behind.

He had one more shot and she was in the way, Caroline realised in dismay. Their attackers had not been able to shoot safely before, for fear of hitting one another, but that no longer applied with the two at the rear disposed of.

Swiftly and expertly, she turned her horse aside, forcing it up the bank and across the ditch. Over her shoulder she saw one of the approaching riders veer to come after her as the other aimed his own pistol and fired at Robert.

Caroline was struggling to get the second pistol from the holster, and with a gasp of triumph she brought it out. From the corner of her eye she saw Robert's horse stumble and fall slowly to the ground. There was the sound of another shot, but she could not tell whose it was, or see if it hit its target.

She had no time to watch, and with a cry of anguish turned her pistol towards the man riding straight for her. He was almost on her, but her one thought was to avenge Robert. She halted her horse, took steady aim, and fired.

This time she did not close her eyes. This time she wanted to hit the target, and to her immense satisfaction she saw him rock in the saddle as the bullet hit him full in the chest. Then he was gone, clinging to the saddle as his horse galloped away.

Fearful of what she would find, Caroline rode back to the edge of the road where she'd last seen Robert's horse falling as the remaining attacker thundered down towards him.

Robert's horse was on the ground, twitching in agony, but Robert had vaulted free of the stirrups and drawn his sword. His adversary, also with drawn sword, but still mounted, circled round to try and find an opening. Caroline watched in frustration. The mounted man had an almost unbreakable advantage over them both, with Robert on foot and her only remaining weapon the small dagger she had earlier thrust into her boot.

There would be no time to get Robert mounted on her horse, so somehow she had to try to unseat the robber. But how could she achieve that?

11

Caroline looked round for inspiration. There had been four men, all mounted. Two were dead, the one she'd wounded had been carried away by his horse, so where were the other horses? To her increasing excitement she saw one grazing peacefully a short distance away. An idea emerged.

She walked her own horse slowly towards the loose one. It edged away slightly, but when she halted, it resumed grazing. The second time she tried to approach, it merely lifted its head to look at her, and by calling gently to it she was able to come alongside.

The reins hung slackly and she gathered them up close under the bit. The horse permitted her to lead it down on to the track. She turned back to where Robert was still fending off the robber's attack and trying to dislodge him from the saddle.

Caroline dug in her heels and urged her horse into a gallop as quickly as she could, the other horse pounding alongside. She bore down on the two men, knowing that Robert was facing her and aware of her intention.

His adversary turned when she gave a sudden shout. At that moment Robert ducked under his sword and grasped him by the arm, hauling him from the saddle as Caroline swept past.

She had some difficulty in halting the excited horses. When she turned to look, she found the two men fighting on foot, the robber's horse circling worriedly beyond them.

By now it was dusk and becoming difficult to distinguish what was happening at even a short distance. The men were evenly matched, but Robert had been fighting on foot for a considerable time. He was moving slowly and Caroline was desperately afraid he might have been injured.

As she watched, wondering whether a further intervention would help or hinder Robert, she heard the sound of trotting hooves behind her. Thank goodness, some other late traveller whose presence might scare away the robber.

'Help!' she called, and turned to peer through the gathering dusk at the newcomer. 'Come quickly, please! We're being attacked!' she called again.

Why didn't he speak? She could distinguish the big, powerful horse, and the military bearing of the rider, but no details. She went closer, intending to urge him on, but suddenly his hand shot out and he caught her by the wrist.

'So, pretty little Caroline, I thought I'd come across you somewhere on this road. But you've taken an uncommon time getting here. Was it pleasant dallying with Royalist scum on the way?'

'John Culham! You followed us all this way? These ruffians are your men?' she exclaimed in horror.

She began to struggle, but he was far too strong for her. Within minutes he dragged her across the pommel of his saddle. With her stomach pressed painfully against the hard edge, and her hands held behind her in a cruel grip, she could only kick fiercely, but her efforts were futile.

'We'll soon have the truth out of your cavalier,' Culham said mockingly, turning to ride away. 'I guessed you'd head for Falmouth. We'd only to watch the most likely roads. My men will soon overpower him and bring him after us.'

'Your men are dead, apart from that one!' Caroline said with grim satisfaction. 'And with his greater skill with the sword, Robert will soon send him to join them!'

'What touching faith you have in him!'

Caroline prayed she was right. When she heard the sound of hooves galloping after them she redoubled her silent pleas. Robert, though hard pressed, had seen the new arrival and heard

Caroline's protests. Since the start of the ambush he'd suspected it was more than just a casual robbery. It was too well organised.

Caroline's exclamation confirmed this suspicion. It gave him the added spur. Suddenly he swung his sword in a rapid movement that deceived his opponent who found his own weapon inexplicably torn from his grasp.

He had but a few moments to wonder how it had happened before Robert drove his blade through the other's heart, then, not waiting for him to collapse, raced to leap on the back of the loose horse and set off after Culham and Caroline.

Culham glanced back and realised it was not one of his men coming up fast behind him. With his double load he could not hope to outdistance the other, and with a curse, he flung Caroline down and set spurs to his horse.

* * *

When Caroline awoke, her head was aching violently. She opened her eyes but did not recognise the room. Where was she, and what had happened? She sighed, closed her eyes and tried to will the pain away.

Some time later, when she tried to move, she realised that her body ached even more than her head. With another sigh she abandoned the struggle and retreated back into sleep.

It was the following day before she was fit to talk. The innkeeper's wife who tended her, friendly and curious, came into the room in some excitement. She helped her sit up, insisted on combing Caroline's hair, and said the gentleman was wishful of a few minutes with her if she felt well enough.

'What gentleman?' Caroline demanded warily, recollection flooding back. 'Where am I? What happened?'

'The gentleman who brought you here, of course,' the woman replied soothingly, but Caroline became more agitated.

'No, who, which one?' she persisted, but the woman had gone.

Caroline shrank back against the pillows, and then remembered the dagger in her boot. What had become of it? She stumbled out of bed, and realised the nightgown she wore must belong to the woman she had seen. It was far too long and voluminous for her.

Clutching it awkwardly in her arms she looked hastily round the room. Her clothes were folded neatly on a stool, the boots placed tidily underneath. She threw the clothes to the floor, and gave a sob of relief to find her dagger underneath. Seizing it, she held it in front of her and turned to the door as the latch clicked.

Slowly, agonisingly slowly it seemed to Caroline, the latch lifted. She watched it tensely, and stepped back as the door swung open, holding her dagger in front of her.

'Do you always greet me with a weapon?' Robert queried lazily.

With a sob Caroline flung herself across the room, stumbling over the hem of the nightgown, and fell into his arms.

'I thought it might be him!' she gasped. 'John Culham. What happened? Are you hurt? Did you fight him? He threw me off the horse,' she recalled.

'Yes, and the fall stunned you for a while. Caroline, my love, I am made intensely nervous while you wave that dagger about. Could you bear to let me have it?'

She gave a weak laugh.

'Here it is. I'm sorry. But what happened? Did you catch him?' she demanded.

'Yes, and he'll trouble us no more, dear Caroline. I don't know if the one you shot got away. There have been no reports of another wounded man being found. Have you been practising your shooting secretly, by the way?'

'No, I have not! And I only hit you because I shut my eyes when I fired,' she said indignantly. 'This time I meant it. I really wanted to kill him!'

'How bloodthirsty you've become! And how fortunate for me. It was a dangerous nest of Roundhead vipers we wiped out between us,' he added with a chuckle. 'If they'd won, heaven knows what damage they could have done here, and the Prince is heading this way soon. Now, my dear, ought you not to be in bed? I'm sure you're still not well enough to be cavorting about the room!'

Suddenly aware that not only was she in a borrowed nightgown, but also clasped tightly in his arms, Caroline blushed furiously and moved swiftly back.

'I'm so sorry!' she mumbled. 'I was just so relieved it wasn't him! The landlady didn't tell me who it was.'

She scrambled hastily into bed and pulled the covers well up to her chin.

'So it was relief rather than joy at seeing me? I'm not flattered,' he said smoothly.

She looked at him suspiciously, and

decided it was a strange form of humour she could not understand. Her head must be worse than it felt.

'How did you beat him?' she asked, to keep her true emotions under control.

'The first I disarmed, and took his horse. Culham was a poor swordsman,' he said calmly. 'He lasted but five minutes. When they were both dealt with I found you, and brought you to the inn at Columb. That was two days ago.'

'When must we start for Falmouth? Have you sent for Henry Waring?'

'No, I thought it best to wait until you were feeling more yourself. We needn't go until you're quite ready. And now, my dear, I think you should sleep.'

She was immensely tired, but before she slept she dwelt on those few precious moments when she'd been clasped in his arms. She wanted to imprint the feel of his body, the outdoor, heathery scent of him, on herself. It would be all she had to remember him by.

* * *

Two days later she'd recovered quite enough to travel. Robert had spent the time rounding up the loose horses from the moor nearby. He recovered Caroline's own mount, and two belonging to the Roundheads. One of the captured animals replaced his own mount, which had been shot, and the innkeeper was delighted to accept the other beast. His own riding horse had been commandeered by the Royalist army two years since.

They rode in silence for much of the day, but Robert insisted that they ride slowly with many halts for Caroline to have some rest. They passed through Truro around noon, and when they came in sight of the river, with the port of Falmouth spread out in front of them, Robert suggested a last stop.

He lifted Caroline down gently from

her horse, as he had insisted on doing all day, saying she was still quite delicate. They tethered the horses and sat looking across the estuary, the water grey under the pale winter sky.

'When will you be going?' Caroline asked softly. 'Will you be able to find a ship?'

'There's a friendly fisherman always ready to take me across to France,' he replied. 'I use this route often.'

Caroline wondered if she would ever see him again. It seemed unlikely. The war was probably over, the King defeated, and he would have little cause to return to England.

'I wish you well,' she said quietly.

'If the boat is ready I mean to sail tonight,' he said.

He turned towards her and took her hand in his.

'Caroline, if I return soon, is there any hope you would come back with me to France?'

'With you?' she repeated, feeling numb with surprise.

Then a wave of fury hit her and she snatched her hand away.

'Caroline,' he began, but she rushed into speech.

'As your mistress, presumably? Why else would you ask me? No, Lord Ashring, I will be no man's mistress! Go and marry your duke's daughter, but don't expect me to provide entertainment for your leisure hours!'

'Caroline! What duke's daughter? What the plague are you talking about?'

'The one to whom you are betrothed.'

'Who on earth told you that?'

'So you didn't intend me to know? Thank goodness Mistress Somerton mentioned it or I might have misunderstood you! And now please let go of my hand. You're hurting me, and it is time we moved on!'

'We're staying here until we've sorted this out. Julia has been causing trouble, has she? Caroline, I'm not betrothed to anyone, let alone a duke's daughter.'

'But she said so!'

'Never mind what she said. Julia cannot resist trying to make trouble. You'll listen to me. I've never before asked anyone to marry me, but that's what I'm doing now. I want you to come to France with me, as my wife. I love you, have been driven demented with the desire to take you in my arms and make you mine ever since I saw you in that doorway, aiming your pistol at me.'

She stared at him, unable to speak. Her heart was so incredibly full she thought she would burst with happiness.

'I'm not asking you to decide immediately, for I suppose this is unexpected. I'll return to you here as soon as I've reported to the Queen in France, and I hope you will have been able to decide by then. Caroline, my dear beloved, I want you so much, can you give me any hope at all?'

'But, Robert, I didn't think you loved me! I thought it was hopeless! And please, don't leave me here! Why should

I stay? I want to come with you now! I don't ever want to lose you, be away from you again!'

Oblivious of a party of riders passing by he took her into his arms, and she melted into them as if they'd always been around her.

For the first time since she had ever set eyes on him, she could give and receive his loving kisses joyfully, with no doubts whatever of his intentions.

When she'd shot her cavalier it had been the luckiest shot of the war.

THE END

Other titles in the
Linford Romance Library:

THREE TALL TAMARISKS

Christine Briscomb

Joanna Baxter flies from Sydney to run her parents' small farm in the Adelaide Hills while they recover from a road accident. But after crossing swords with Riley Kemp, life is anything but uneventful. Gradually she discovers that Riley's passionate nature and quirky sense of humour are capturing her emotions, but a magical day spent with him on the coast comes to an abrupt end when the elegant Greta intervenes. Did Riley love Greta after all?

SUMMER IN HANOVER SQUARE

Charlotte Grey

The impoverished Margaret Lambart is suddenly flung into all the glitter of the Season in Regency London. Suspected by her godmother's nephew, the influential Marquis St. George, of being merely a common adventuress, she has, nevertheless, a brilliant success, and attracts the attentions of the young Duke of Oxford. However, when the Marquis discovers that Margaret is far from wanting a husband he finds he has to revise his estimate of her true worth.

CONFLICT OF HEARTS

Gillian Kaye

Somerset, at the end of World War I: Daniel Holley, unhappily married to an ailing wife and father of four grown-up children, is attracted to beautiful schoolteacher Harriet Bray, but he knows his love is hopeless. Daniel's only daughter, Amy, who dreams of becoming a milliner and is caught up in her love for young bank clerk John Tottle, looks on as the drama of Daniel and Harriet's fate and happiness gradually unfolds.

THE SOLDIER'S WOMAN

Freda M. Long

When Lieutenant Alain d'Albert was deserted by his girlfriend, a replacement was at hand in the shape of Christina Calvi, whose yearning for respectability through marriage did not quite coincide with her profession as a soldier's woman. Christina's obsessive love for Alain was not returned. The handsome hussar married an heiress and banished the soldier's woman from his life. But Christina was unswerving in the pursuit of her dream and Alain found his resistance weakening . . .